BROKEN LINKS
MENDED LIVES

ROCKY MOUNTAIN
FICTION WRITERS

© 2009 RMFW Press
BROKEN LINKS, MENDED LIVES
ISBN 0-9760225-2-4

At Fenwick Faire ©2009 Carol Berg
Flowers For Amelia ©2009 Cindi Myers
The Prince and Broken Water ©2009 Rebecca Rowley
I Love Lucy ©2009 Curtis Craddock
Devastation Mine ©2009 Nikki Baird
Opportunity Howls ©2009 Barb A. Smith
The Nu Tao Café ©2009 Judy Metz
Porter ©2009 Alexei Kalinchuk
The Cowgirl and the Plum Crazy Purple B ©2009 Jameson Cole
Leaving the Light ©2009 Rebecca S.W. Bates
A Long Way ©2009 Susan G. Fisher
Water Monster ©2009 Mario Acevedo
The Wind Has Blown the Leaves Away ©2009 William M. Brock
Lonely Crutch ©2009 Terry Kroenung
Weaving Money ©2009 Liz Hill

RMFW Press
P.O. Box 545
Englewood, CO 80151
www.rmfw.org

Cover design by Jalena Penaligon
Interior design by Duvall Design
Printed in the United States of America
123456789

Table of Contents

Dedication

With heartfelt gratitude, the editors dedicate this anthology to the selection jury, all published authors in Rocky Mountain Fiction Writers, who chose the stories: Mario Acevedo, Kay Bergstrom, Christine Jorgensen, Chris Goff, Warren Hammond, Shannon Baker, Mark Stevens, Terry Banker, Susan Hornick, Mary Gillgannon, Tina Ann Forkner, Kathleen Elbinger, Jeff Shelby, Linda Berry, and Carol Caverly. Our deepest thanks for the exceptional work of Jalena Penaligon, Karen Duvall, Linda Berry, and Carol Caverly, without which we could not have produced this book.

Introduction

Arthur Conan Doyle once remarked, "there are far fewer supremely good short stories than there are supremely good long books. It takes more exquisite skill to carve the cameo than the statue."

Rocky Mountain Fiction Writers is pleased to present fifteen exquisite cameos.

We begin with *At Fenwick Faire* by award-winning author Carol Berg, a serious fantasy of redemption and renewal.

It is followed by an unusual love story by Cindi Myers; a moving, funny story about an unwed eighteen-year-old about to deliver her first baby and still awaiting her "prince" by Rebecca Rowley; Curtis Craddock's sly, multilayered time-travel story; a Colorado ghost story by Nikki Baird; Barb A. Smith's hilarious tale about a team-builder who takes on an unusual *pack* of clients; Judy Metz's frothy piece about a newly-divorced woman who, with the help of a dog she didn't want and the ancient Chinese crone who runs the Nu Tao Café, fixes her life.

Alexei Kalinchuk gives us a literary slice-of-life; Jameson Cole action and romance during the Greeley Stampede; Rebecca S. W. Bates a mystical and powerful science fiction story about a space pilot's duty and the changes it demands of her; a "pay-it-forward" story from Susan G. Fisher.

We have Mario Acevedo's quirky fantasy which turns our theme of *Broken Links, Mended Lives* on its head; William M. Brock's keen reflections on life and the demi-monde of art and music clubs in which a nowhere guy's body is taken over by a ghost who has more of a life than his host; and Terry Kroenung's remarkable twist on a well-known Dickens character.

Our last story, *Weaving Money* by Liz Hill, details the experiences of two expectant mothers in different corners of the globe and how their lives intersect in an unexpected way.

All wonderful, all original, all well-crafted stories showcasing the talent in this organization. Rocky Mountain Fiction Writers is proud to present this third anthology. We hope you not only enjoy the stories, but will be inspired to follow the careers of these talented writers to discover what other jewels they have written.

Janet Lane
Susan Mackay Smith
Jeanne C. Stein
Editors

At Fenwick Faire
by Carol Berg

My parents never told me I had Talent. Perhaps they thought it undignified for the daughter of a city magistrate, or believed it might frighten me or make me insolent. Or maybe they just left it too late, and had the lack of consideration to die of plague before warning me.

Now don't think me unfeeling, but when one is ten years old and the whole world is dying of plague, or slaughtering each other for fear of it, or taking flight to escape it, one has little time to mourn, or even to recall why one should. When civilization has erupted into chaos, the next meal looms much larger in importance than past grieving.

Six years I spent scrabbling in search of that next meal before I trudged up a rock-blasted hill and through the iron gate of Fenwick Priory. By that time I had seen far more of men and life than was really necessary, and taking up residence with a group of similarly exhausted women seemed sensible. The sisterhood grew vegetables, kept to themselves, and did no good works to speak of. I had no illusion that this would be a permanent situation. The sisters didn't seem that agreeable, and entanglement of any sort made me want to cram a shiv in someone's craw.

"You'll tend a plot, Girl," said the bony Prioress, licking the beaded honey from a suckle blossom grown right out of the crumbled courtyard wall. "Each of us has one."

"Don't know how," I said and scratched my itchy foot on a cracked step. "Not opposed, but I never learnt. My parents called planting hireling's work. I'll scrub for you. Fetch and carry. Steal, if you want. I'm good at those."

"You don't tend a plot, you don't eat. Go or stay, as you will."

I stayed. The road had got tiresome of late. My boots had fallen to pieces, and a thieving tallyman had jacked my knife. Bare hands or sticks weren't enough to fend off the skags, now I was ripe. Last thing I needed was a squaller planted inside me. My own belly was empty half the time.

Early on my second morning, Prioress marched me down the long valley back of the priory, past twenty or so vegetable patches. "Choose," she said, waving her hand around the empty scrubland.

I didn't know squat about gardens, but I walked about and settled on a spot. "Here."

With sticks and knotted string pulled from dead women's dresses, the Prioress staked out a square of hard gray dirt. "There's wood in the shed and a chisel to make your tools. When you're ready to plant, we've seed stock in the vault."

One of the sisters, digging nearby, mopped her sweat and snickered. She sounded like the cicadas rasping in the dry brush. "Can't eat the weeds, stupid Girl. Got to pull them before you can plant. You just chose yourself more work."

So I had. Spiky thistles and snarls of threadweed littered my plot. Thistles would sting, and tough, fibery threadweed would cut my hands, but it made sense that if something grew there now, something other might.

To be sure, the cultivated plots roundabout looked little better. Stunted beans. Wilted greens. The sisters saved them from parched oblivion by hauling water from a nearby stream, doling it out drop by precious drop. The stream itself was scarce but a trickle of spit.

You see, our land had been thirty years without rain. Lots of folk had survived the famines, the plague, and the wars, only to succumb to despair at the endless withering. City people said the desert was reclaiming its own, that the two hundred years of generous moisture had been the aberration. The pious said the drought was punishment from the gods for the decadent ways of the cities. The Rounders, scorned by the civilized, said our decline was merely the cycle of the Guardians, and that the rain would return when the Wheel came round again. I named them all lackwits to imagine there was a reason to it, and crazier still when they claimed that those with Talents would figure out the cure for it.

In the winter just past, I had reached my sixteenth birthday, that time when Talent begins to manifest itself. I was glad I'd none to fret about. If the Birth-Seeing reveals you as having Talent, loving parents or tutors can read the signs that mark you as a Healer, Warrior, Spellcaster, or whatever, and help you nurture your gift slow and easy. But without anyone to help, you must muddle through the unsettling years, trying this or that, waiting until the Talent bursts out whole in pain and blood, like a babe from the womb. Mostly, by that time, you're too old for apprenticing, too unskilled for employment, and too ignorant to shape the future to your will. I'd seen folk go crazy from it.

And what was the use after all? Healers had produced no cure for plague. Warriors with flaming swords might frighten wild hillmen, but could not keep a randy soldier's hand from under your skirt. And nary a Spellcaster had ever conjured a drop of rain. The world was just dry. We were all going to die of it. Now or then. Didn't matter which.

I set to work that first afternoon, watching the other sisters about their plots and taking on the problem of making my square of dirt look more like theirs. I poked at the soil with a stick from the woodpile. Picked out stones and cleared out threadweed and thistles until my hands bled. Hauled dung from the sties down by the village, as some of them did. Seemed logical to feed the land you wanted to feed you back.

A tenday of digging and hauling, and the color of the soil had deepened to a rich brown. Prioress nodded and gave me seeds, debting me to return them threefold.

Plant, tend, dig, turn. Haul the water, and drip it careful. The cycle was clean and uncomplicated, and from the first I understood the way of it absolutely. Logic. Wholeness. A tenday more, and my seedlings burst out and shook off the dirt like a whore shakes off her last customer of the night. In all my years scrounging through rubble and refuse, I'd never imagined a pleasure could be found from grubbing in the dirt.

When the heat began to wither my plants, I dug deep down where the soil was cooler and found a spring buried underneath the garden. I pulled out rocks and kept the soil loose, so the roots could find it. I had always been lucky finding water. The skill was stored up inside me right along with the best way to snatch an apple from a market cart and the easiest method of lifting a fine gentleman's wallet.

The sisters mumbled to each other about how fat my beans grew despite the drought. If they'd asked, I could have told them the same spring sat right underneath their own garden plots. But six years on the road had left me little accustomed to going out of my way to inform the ignorant. A raft of knife scars and fright dreams reminded me of those first days back when I was ten and the world was collapsing around me. I'd tried to join up with others wandering, thinking someone would take care of me. I'd learned hard.

Still, Prioress came to me one day. Poked at my plants with her shabby boot. "Hey, Girl. Some say you're taking more than your share of the stream water. We'll take a whip to you for that."

"Watch me," I said, shoving her boot away. "I take less." And she did, and agreed I was fair.

Took me three days to believe I'd not walked away at the first rumbling of trouble. My back carried whip marks enough for three lifetimes. Prioress was a big woman. Hard. With help to hold me, she could likely have done what she said. But I'd knifed the last person tried whipping me—a skag who wanted me to serve his pleasure—and killing left a sour belly and a bitter taste in the mouth. Wasn't worth it.

As the Priory summer drifted by, the old restlessness stirred in me till I thought I must move on or burst. I needed to find someplace cleaner. Away from arid souls and scabby ruins. I'd not stayed in one place so long since I'd abandoned my parents' corpses in our burning house, since the pretty, pampered child I was had become scavenger, thief, whore, and worse, all to keep on breathing. But that square of dirt shackled my feet. I just couldn't abandon my sturdy plants until I witnessed their full fruitfulness. So I vowed to stay on through harvest. Not a day longer.

#

At the peak of the harvest, when our bellies bulged with fresh beans, carrots, and greens, came time for Fenwick Faire. Each year the sisters took their excess produce to the faire to trade for wool and tea, flour, pepper, and oil.

Having so recently shed the company of people in general, and men in particular, I was tempted to forego the journey. But the restlessness stirred in me, as if I starved and the world's last bread sat waiting at Fenwick Town. So I took my share of my beans and went. At least I might trade for a pair of boots. Pretty soon now, I'd be leaving the Priory for good.

Five of us set off in the smoky grayness before dawn. A chill hung in the air like a hint of wine in water. Straggling wedges of geese crossed the sunrise, heading for the promise of warmth in the south. I could have told them they would find no comfort there.

We dragged our cart into the fairgrounds, a whirlpool of activity in the midst of an arid plain that stretched all the way to the purple hills on the horizon. Vendors hammered together booths and stalls. Townsmen hauled in tables for eating, and marked rings and tracks for sports. Rounders set up tents for gamesters and fortunetellers. In the way of those with short childhoods, I marveled that anyone would think a fortuneteller would say anything other than what the customer wanted to hear. Tell people the truth and they would never pay.

My sack of shelled beans over my shoulder, I left the sisters and wandered about the fairgrounds, intending to complete my business early and be off. A leathery hand plucked at my sleeve, the stubby fingers heavy with rings of fool's diamonds and false gold.

"Your fortune, Girl," came a wheedling voice, raspy and low. "Only a penny and I'll tell you your true love."

I turned to tell the Rounder woman that I had no penny, no fortune, no truth, and assuredly no love for anyone, but her eyes caught me like a hook trap. Brown like garden earth. Deep like a well. Glistening like oil in lamplight. My words flitted away like dandelion fluff on the breeze.

She nodded and grinned. A soiled blue scarf wrapped her greasy hair, and the state of what was left of her teeth would have made me gag had I any morsel of sensibility left in me. She pulled me inside. "Knew you'd come."

The stuffy dimness of her tent stank of smoldering herbs and sour wine. Hard to imagine that stale, reeking air was the same as that outside, sweet with dust and autumn morning.

I ached to bolt, but my will had flown with my words, so when she guided me to a splintered packing crate, I sat docile as a dead man. She perched on a stool behind an oily barrel stood on end, humming to herself. My whole body strained to hear. From a rusty iron box sitting beside her on the floor, she drew a bundle of dirty rags, set it on the barrel end, and unwrapped it one strip of cloth at a time. A pink crystal the size of my fist sat splendid amidst its filthy drapery.

Still crooning, she clapped her small brown hands about the crystal, her heavy rings flashing in the lamplight. Shafts of rosy light pierced the cocoon of her fingers. I would have turned my eyes from the brightness were I able, for in the shadowed corner of the tent, a hollow-eyed child watched us hungrily. Her hair was stringy, and her clothes hung ragged and filthy on her bones. The bruises on her spindly arms throbbed on my own, and I knew the gnawing emptiness inside her.

"Water and Earth," sang the woman, her pent melody breaking into the Rounders' Lay. "Water and Earth, Wind and Fire. The Guardians live, and the Great Wheel turns…" When her song was done, she bent close enough I could smell the garlic on her breath. "Wake up, Girl. Heed the call. Thy return has been foretold since the breaking. My rein be upon thee, bound to my circle until need carries thee to where thy lover waits."

The pink radiance faded. The brown hands buried the crystal in its wrapping once again. The crone sat back in her chair and smiled her ragged smile.

Shaking off my stupor, I snapped my head around. No child stood in that tent.

"Cheap tricks," I said, jumping to my feet. "You're out of luck, old woman, for I've no money, and nothing you would want, and your raving made no sense anyway."

"On the contrary, pretty miss, you have satisfied all my wants. Be off with you."

Just the kind of wretched business I had seen so often, wild-eyed crazies trying to mesmerize the ignorant. Who knew what her game was? Heart galloping, I snatched up my sack, yanked it open, and plunged my hand in. Beans. Not rocks or sand. I'd been lucky.

I flung aside the tent flap, and breathed deep of the dry and dusty warmth outside. The midday sun had sapped the cool of morning. Cookfires had been lit, thin blue trails of smoke rising straight up in the still air. Smells of frying onions and stewing chicken snared my empty stomach with knots of desire.

More of the local populace streamed into the fairgrounds. Children chased each other about the tents and stalls, their dirty bare feet stirring up clouds of dust to settle on the carefully displayed wares. Gaunt farmers and their pinchy wives dickered over sheep and goats that seemed more bone than flesh. The gamesters' tents were filling up with pock-marked young men, each with a year's wages in his pocket, ripe for plucking.

A red-faced farm-wife, sweating over her iron skillet, traded me a half-moon-shaped meat pie for a cupful of my shelled beans. The bargain seemed decent enough until I bit into the few bits of gristle, and my teeth dragged out a brownish clump of onion and cabbage. But I had eaten worse. I finished it, licked the fat from my fingers, and got on about my business.

Nobody had good shoes to sell. Sandals and woolen leggings would have to do for winter. Perhaps the farmers were eating the animal hides rather than tanning them. My beans bought me a bag of blue-dyed wool, a decent knife the length of my hand, and, somewhat inexplicably, a scarf of grass green to tie back my hair. Ordinarily I scoffed at personal adornments, and preferred my hair short, like a man's. But without a good knife, my hair had grown longer, and the scarf appealed to me. The rest of the beans I left with the sisters, who bartered for the Priory stores in which I shared.

Business done, I could shed this press of unwelcome humankind. So why did I not? Through the sweltering stillness of the afternoon, I wandered about the fairgrounds, searching for some thing I could not name. Unease swelled within me like a cyclone birthing.

When the shadows began to lengthen, the wind came up. Dust devils danced across the plains beyond the fairgrounds, whirling crazy like the Afflicted, back in the years smut blighted the rye. The hot canvas tents flapped and billowed in the dry gusts. Families began to round up strayed children and dogs and pack up their wagons for the long trip back to their lonely farms. Only drinkers and gamblers would be left to light the lamps and pursue the more raucous pleasures of the evening.

Still I tarried. Most likely the sisters had gone already, not expecting me to outstay them. A lone woman on the roads at night best have a quick knife and quicker feet. But no matter peril, no matter sense, I could not go.

My restless wandering led me to the deserted edge of the fairgrounds, where I perched on a grease-spattered plank table and watched the onset of night. The bloated sun, red in the dust haze, sagged below the distant hills. The gusts off the lifeless plains grew cold. Heat lightning flickered false promises in the bowl of the sky.

Harsh laughter, the familiar tenor of tavern and alleyway, burst from the gaming tents now and then, while whispering pairs of figures darted from the tents into the deeper shadows nearby. The giggling and sighs spoke only of wretched fumbling, stinking bodies, and emptiness.

I had thought all grieving left behind me in the wreckage of my childhood, but the chill within me on this night was no less than that without. I wrapped my arms about myself tightly to crush the swelling hurt. Still it grew, as if I were that starving child in the Rounder's tent. So, after a time, not understanding at all what it was I did, I stood up on the table, lifted my arms to the wind and the jagged pink fire in the sky, and cried out desolation.

Roaring thunder burst from the sky, and clouds blacker than the desert night boiled up over the hills and blotted out the stars. Lightning ripped the heavens as if to set the earth ablaze. I flung my arms over my head as the night exploded around me. I expected to be swept away like so much straw. But the whirlwind wrapped me in flickering cloud, lifted me up, and pushed back the storm to leave me in … another place.

Clouds smoothed and shaped themselves into a ring of carved pillars, a domed ceiling, and a vast patterned floor of swirling gray and white. Beyond the ring of pillars lay naught but night, cloud, and lightning. But in its center sat a broad desk. A man sat beside it on a stool, poring over a wide scroll, dipping his quill in an ink bottle and sketching details into a drawing—mountains the shape of cones, lakes like cups, houses that appeared to be … rings of pillars.

"Who are you?" I said, fear cinching my throat. "What is this place?" Perhaps the meat pie had poisoned me. Perhaps I was Afflicted and would die clawing my own skin away.

The man whirled around and leaped to his feet, setting the lightning beyond the pillars crackling. "You've come!"

Never had I seen a man of such striking appearance. His eyes were green fire, his windblown hair the color of midnight sky, his radiant face the hue of rich earth—unscarred, intelligent, pleasing in a way that caused my belly to quiver. Clean. A simple tunic left little guessing as to his form, all lean, rangy limbs.

I backed away. I knew pretty men. Skags, all of them.

Wind skirled and whined through the pillars, rattling his scroll in its clamps. Reining his moment's exuberance, the man bowed to me. When he raised up, his fire-touched gaze remained lowered, his dusky skin flushed. "I've been waiting so very long," he said with a stern, quiet grace. "For you, I think. Only you in all the world."

My hand flew to my knife sheath. "Not I. No man waits for me nor ever will. What's your name?"

"I cannot remember." His brow wrinkled, puzzled. His ink-stained fingers riffled his hair. "So many seasons have passed. But I do not believe it matters. You're the Gardener, yes? Come to lie with me?"

Loathing tightened my fists, and I bolted for the opening between two pillars. False innocence could hide the worst vileness.

The rippling lightning stung my arms as I plunged into the cloud. This seeming was but charweed smoke or some food-borne poison affecting my sight and skin. I would find some tent or wagon to hide behind, stick my finger down my throat, and puke it up.

"Wait! You cannot go until you answer! Please!"

But his distant cry did not slow me, and I ran until a pool of gray light opened before me...

My racing heart seized. I stood inside the circle of pillars again.

Twice more I ran. Twice more the path led me back. Fear and rage trembled my limbs. "Are you a Spellcaster?"

"I'm not—"

"Never was a Spellcaster wasn't a toad-eating villain. Leave me be!"

"To leave here, you must answer yea or nay. No, please wait!" He extended a hand, and his will sealed my refusal before I could speak it. "So many need what we can give. If we could just talk a little. Come to know each other. I think we've met before."

As he stepped away from his stool, a steely clatter drew my eye to his bare foot. A chain shackled his ankle. Its other end lay hid beneath the patterned floor.

"Why are you chained?" I said, shaking. The wind howled, shredding the clouds, offering glimpses of a star-riddled night sky.

"I offered. The land starved, and the templar said I had the Gift to become … this. And the patience to wait for the Gardener. And the strength to be alone. Though when they bound me naked in the storm, I did not fully understand. How could I?" Turning to his desk, he stoppered his ink and gently tapped his fluttering scroll, clamped tight at either end against the wind. "My memory fades. I fear that most."

"Templar?" The word echoed faintly from beneath the detritus of chaos. I had been schooled those few years before the plague, when I knew naught of dirt or ugliness. "Three thousand years have gone since templars ruled."

You'd have thought I'd slapped him. "Three thousand—? Then you've come to me before. Surely. Elsewise all the world would be long dead." Unsteady reasoning fueled his moment's panic.

Eyes afire with the wild lightning, he tore at his scroll, unwinding its leftward length, running his long, stained fingers over his drawing. I edged closer, peering through the wavering light.

"There!" He lifted his face, and relief shone through him as moonlight through a veil. "See?" He held the scroll open, his posture, his certainty, his joy drawing me near enough to see, close enough to inhale his sweet scent, the scent of rain that awakened memory…

I knew him.

His drawing affirmed it. Though I had spent little time mirror gazing since I was ten, who would not recognize her own hands? He had even inked in my green scarf on his page.

Shock and fright yielded to astonishment. Time and remembrance twined and shifted. I always found a green scarf to wear when I came to meet him anew, so he would recognize me after so long. As together we remembered each other. His shy laugh. My bold teasing. His ink-stained fingers, so long and graceful and tender. My everlasting wonder at his giving, and my delight at giving back to him in turn. The sweetness of our passion.

And there, in the eye of the hurricane, was my Talent recalled to me, and my choice again made plain. A Gardener I was, but of much more than a few short rows of beans. The earth itself was in my hand. I knew him, and knew that he was intended for me from the beginning of time until the end, should I but choose it so. Again and again, as I had chosen before. To lie with him. To love him…

But never had I come to him as I was now. "I cannot," I whispered, averting my eyes, my breath trapped in the thorns of my heart. "Not this time. You cannot know how it is in the world now. Worse than ever before, I think. I am filthy. Ugly. Scarred, inside and out. I've forgotten how."

"Do not answer yet," he said softly, reaching for my hand before I could step too far away. "Let us walk a little." He slipped the scroll into a rack that appeared at his hand and vanished when he had done with it.

In a moment, or an hour, or a moon's turn—I could not say which—he shared with me his millennia of solitude. His chain stretched to the pillars, and through each portal he displayed for me his realm of air and cloud, of rippling light and darkness, of scintillating color and fiery wonder. Through one gap, we saw mountains, fields, valleys and palaces of white cloud, lit by stars and crescent moon hung in an ebon sky. In another a comet crossed the sky, its tail of ice brilliant blues and greens. All that I had sought without knowing it stretched before me. I thought I would never tire of the glory, such peace, such wild beauty

… reflected so wondrously in him who revealed it.

"Now you," he said as we sat at the verge of his prison. His back rested on a pillar of shaped cloud. My feet dangled into a whirlwind. "I would remember what I have forsaken."

I was shamed to tell him of my sordid life and despairing world. But to my amazement he relished each detail, treasured each word of bird and tree and seedling, of thief and beggar and poet, of child's game, crumbling city, and struggling farm, of encounters and escapes. To see such variety, to feel the substance of earth and leaf and stone again would be marvelous to him, he said. And to know other beings, to hear and speak and touch…

But he had chosen his fate long ago. He was bound to his world of wind and fire, its Guardian, yet he yearned for the touch of grass and flesh. And I, who longed for purity and light, some escape from my base existence, was bound likewise to the humble earth.

I raged. I, who needed no one, to be beloved¾to abandon my independence, my self, for responsibility on such a scale. To be a Guardian was to freely choose the bondage I detested, over and over again. The price of the land's healing was love and ever-grieving.

"I cannot choose you. Not again. Not this time." Better to forget forever the beauty that he was, than to know it so far out of reach.

But when my explosion of anger and fear was spent, the one who stood beside me stroked my hair. "I remember this," he said, smiling shyly in his way. "You always argue. You never recognize your own beauty. But the Gift is in you, and you always give. Your chain is stronger than mine."

He was right, of course. My first seedling had been the master link in my own chain, a chain of hollow-eyed children and blighted fields and plague-wasted lives. I had forged its length myself.

Setting my foot upon the way offered me, I touched his proffered hand and allowed his smile to pierce my armored heart.

There would be no miraculous joining of our separate paths. The lot of the Guardians was not so. Yet even afterward, as the wind rocked me in my lover's arms, and the cold and lonely lightning played upon his face, as if to mock me with all I must leave behind, I could not regret my choice. At long last, the blessed rain began to fall.

When I again became aware of the world about me, the tempest had given way to a gentle, constant shower. Soaked and shivering, I knelt on the plank table in the midnight darkness. The damp breeze caressed my cheek and stroked my dripping hair. Then ... oh yes, then did I grieve.

The fairgoers had come out of the tents and looked with awe upon the rain. Some knelt in the mud, some prayed, some lifted their arms and wept with joy, and others made signs against evil. No one seemed to notice me. None asked why my tears were fraught with sorrow. And what could I have told them? That I had coupled with the wind and the lightning? That the fruit of our joining would be their own renewal?

I climbed down from my perch and started for home.

Every year I return to the Faire. Every year the old Rounder smiles her ragged smile as she sees me wander through the tents and displays. And every year my true love comes to meet me there. Only one night a year do the worlds of the Guardians meet, and only then can I soothe his loneliness, and he mine.

Through the days in between I tend my garden and teach my sisters of springs and logic and wholeness, and I listen for his voice in his passion and sorrow and sweetness. His fingers tenderly ruffle my hair, and in sighing breezes he whispers to me his yearning. I've come to believe I have the better part. I think I am lucky to walk my days in this plague-filled world, to plunge my arms into the richness of the earth, and savor the noise and stinks of life. Meanwhile, the rains continue and the land is blessed, until the day the Great Wheel comes round again.

It would have been nice to be warned.

Carol Berg

Carol Berg is a former software engineer who can't quite believe her personal story. Since her 2000 debut with Transformation, *she's been flown to Israel, taught writing in the US, Canada, and Scotland, and become an RMFW Writer of the Year. Her ten epic fantasy novels have won the Geffen, the Prism, and multiple Colorado Book Awards, and have been published in seven languages. Carol's latest novels,* Flesh and Spirit *and* Breath and Bone, *together won the 2009 Mythopoeic Fantasy Award. Kirkus Reviews calls* Breath and Bone *"Absolutely superior."*

Flowers For Amelia
by Cindi Myers

Amelia loved flowers. She wore them in her hair and pinned in bunches at her waist or throat. She would go without lunch for the sake of buying a bouquet to grace her dinner table, and I had known her to stop the car alongside a busy highway to gather armfuls of wild poppies, burying her face in the profusion of crimson blooms, like a pollen-starved butterfly, ecstatic at such sudden abundance.

"When I die, I want the church to be *filled* with flowers," she had told me once. "And I want them to drape my coffin with wreaths of roses." She lay back on the grass, arms across her chest, a mocking, beautiful corpse. Then she smiled and opened her eyes. "I expect your wreath to be the largest, Johnny, or I'll want to know why." She winked then, a gesture that always sent a shiver along my spine. "I intend to be watching you all from above," she said, and then laughed an Amelia-laugh, the wild revel of some other-world spirit.

Does she laugh like that still? I thought as I stood in the flower shop, staring at the buckets of daffodils and daisies and carnations dyed in every hue. Will she even remember me, or care that I brought her flowers?

It had been forty years since I'd seen her last, thirty years since I'd tried my best to capture that wild spirit. But Amelia had made up her mind to live alone, and I wasn't strong enough to fight her. After a while I moved away, and married someone else. I didn't often think about Amelia, except at odd times when I caught the scent of Jungle Gardenia or saw a woman with flowers in her hair.

"Can I help you with something?" The florist's voice pulled me from my memories. I blinked at the buckets of flowers, at the condensation beading on their plastic sides. "Do you have any roses?" I asked.

I bought a dozen roses, pink because pink was always her favorite color. Does she still like pink? I wondered.

I had the florist box the flowers, and I carried them out to my car. As I laid the long white box on the seat beside me, I debated turning around and going home.

But then, I'd already paid for the roses, and what would I do with them if I didn't take them to Amelia?

I drove slowly toward the address her niece had given me, rehearsing in my mind what I would say. *What if she doesn't remember me?* I thought.

I found the number and pulled into the parking lot, then sat for a long time, staring at the softly illuminated sign. "Terrace Hills Nursing Center."

My palms were sweating, my heart racing like a teenager on his first date. Finally I forced myself to get out of the car and walk up to the entrance. I made my way down a tiled hallway, past several women hunched in wheelchairs, their eyes burning into me as I approached. I nodded hello and one of them returned the gesture, while another stretched out a thin, veined hand as if to clutch my coat. I almost turned and ran then, but I forced myself to keep going.

Her niece had told me her room number, but I found I did not really need it. The scent of Jungle Gardenia drifted to me, and when I peeked in the open doorway, I saw her sitting by the window, tending a line of African violets that graced the sill.

"Hello, Amelia," I said, and held my breath, waiting.

She turned and smiled, and I think my heart really did stop a moment, for she was as beautiful as I remembered, though the dark hair was now snowy white and the smooth skin softened with fine lines around her eyes and mouth. "Hello," she said. "Please come in." No recognition in those green eyes, but a great deal of welcome.

"I brought you something," I said, coming over and placing the flower box on her lap.

She looked at me questioningly, then slipped the ribbon from the box and lifted the cover. "Roses!" The cry was one of pure delight, and she bent her head to breathe in the heady fragrance. "Oh, I do love pink roses!"

"Let me find something to put them in," I said, reaching to take them from her.

She waved me away. "Let me look at them a while." She reached over and patted the bed. "Sit down and talk to me." She studied me a moment, eyes searching. "You remind me of someone. But I can't think who."

"It's John," I said. "John Perryman."

Her eyes widened. "Johnny Perryman! But you look so old!" Then she clapped her hand to her mouth and began to laugh, a muffled Amelia laugh, and I felt myself relax a little. "That wasn't a very nice thing to say, was it?" she said.

I smiled. "I can hardly believe it myself when I look in the mirror."

She looked at the roses and reached out to finger a velvety petal. "Amelia, how are you?" I asked.

"Pretty good," she said. "Though someone has taken my car keys, and I can't find them anywhere." She looked up at me. "I'd appreciate it if you'd look for them. How am I going to get to the garden club meeting if I can't find my car keys?"

I was saved from making a reply by the entrance of a pink-smocked aide, who took the roses away in search of a vase. Amelia turned back to the violets and I wondered if she had forgotten I was even in the room with her.

I started to get up and leave, but she turned back to me. "Do you remember, Johnny, the poppies we picked by the road that spring? I had them in vases all over the house."

I nodded. "I remember. I'll never forget how beautiful you looked, surrounded by all those flowers."

She nodded toward the hillside across from her window. "There are poppies that bloom over there in the spring. I can see them from this window." She stood and came and took my hand. "Come walk with me."

I wondered where she'd take me, but it turned out she had a regular route through the building. She held my hand and led me through a maze of corridors, smiling and nodding to the nurses and aides and other residents who greeted her by name, reaching out to pat the hands of those who sat silent in their wheelchairs or stood vacant-eyed in the doorways of their rooms. "I don't know why so many people come here every day," she said. "You'd think they'd have better things to do with their time."

I looked down at her soft white curls, at the place where her scalp showed through the thinning hair, the same delicate pink shade as the roses. I wondered about the brain that lay within that head, at the mind which seemed to be playing hide and seek with me, the old familiar Amelia appearing briefly behind the façade of this other, different woman.

We heard music and followed it to a room I took to be some sort of den or parlor. A young woman was playing the piano and several women and one man sat watching her and listening to the music. I recognized a waltz, one Amelia and I had danced to forty years before.

She squeezed my hand. "Dance with me, Johnny. You always were such a good dancer."

I looked around the room, at the scarred piano and at the man and women with their wheelchairs and walkers. "Here?" I asked.

She smiled up at me. "If you don't dance with me, Johnny, I'll have to ask someone else." Then she winked, and I felt the same shiver up my spine I'd felt all those years ago, when we were both so young, but not, it seemed now, so very different.

I took her in my arms and we waltzed across the tile, in and out among the rows of wheelchairs and walkers. We danced without seeing the room, our eyes locked onto each other, Amelia's hand clasped tightly to mine, my head filled with the scent of gardenias and the memories of our years together and apart.

When I come again, I'll bring a red carnation, I thought. And I'll pin it in her hair. It didn't matter if she remembered me or not; I could remember enough for both of us. Amelia was still Amelia, whose green eyes and laughter gave away her secrets and showed her to be as elusive as she'd ever been for me. And Amelia still loved flowers, almost as much as I loved her.

Cindi Myers, an RMFW Writer of the Year, is the award-winning author of more than 40 romance and women's fiction novels. Find out more about her at www.CindiMyers.com.

The Prince and Broken Water
by Rebecca Rowley

The day my baby was born, I came home from the grocery store and found a note taped to the fridge. The message was short and scribbled over the unpaid phone bill. As I read, my nervous fingers wrestled with my bracelet—the bracelet Luther gave me—until it snapped, a line of silver loops tinkling to the floor.

"I'm sorry," he'd written.

Sorry is the wrong word.

I called voicemail to see if he'd changed his mind and decided to beg me to pick him up from wherever he'd run. Instead, it was just another message from my father. Same one he left every day, ever since I left high school for the twenty-year-old boy next door.

"Britney, it's your father … please … just call me. I need to know you're okay."

How could I call him? *Luther loves me, Daddy. I know he does.*

How could I tell him? *I'm almost eighteen—you can't control my life anymore.*

I kicked away the broken bracelet links and scraped the note off the fridge's door. One folded edge dug into the palm of my hand. I squeezed harder.

He's sorry. Together for a year and now *he's sorry!*

Ripping the note apart, I stepped out into the neighborhood, wandering through the early dark of fall. Pieces of the note littered the sidewalk behind me. I wasn't sure where I was heading; I just let my feet move until my soles said stop. Then I turned my head to the right and stared through the big front window of a restaurant named Rudy's.

From what I could see, Rudy's looked like an Irish pub. Patrons sat inside at round, copper-colored tables. A Hispanic couple wearing bulky sweaters sat by the window and ate sandwiches that were too big for their faces. One guy walked past them and headed for the bar to talk to a brunette waitress with braces on her teeth. She set down a tray of frosty, full steins. *I need water.*

My pregnant body swayed, but I stayed upright. I entered Rudy's through the swinging glass door. The dark wood panels on the walls, the reddish-black floor, and the stamped metal ceiling made the restaurant feel small, like someone's living room. No one looked up to notice me. I wobbled forward and claimed the nearest seat, which happened to be at a table covered with thick books and loose paper.

Guys never clean up their messes.

I pushed one of the books to the center of the table.

Just like Luther's motorcycle magazines. Always spread out over everything—our futon, our tub, his entertainment center. Sometimes he'd lay one over his face while he slept so that only his chiseled chin stuck out.

I tried to sit still, but no position was comfortable. Uneasiness rumbled through my body and sent my pulse into panic mode. My left hand squeezed the fabric of my sweat pants as if it were the last friendly hand to hold.

I can't do this alone.

I quivered. My eyes flooded. I wasn't crying, but my body seemed to be. My skin, my bones, my brain felt so fragile that a warm breath on the back of my neck would have sent me splattering into soggy ashes.

He promised we'd be together. Always together.

The restaurant door sighed as another couple came in. They shuffled off to the corner booth without a glance in my direction—not even when I let out a whimper. My head drooped. A slight weight fell on my shoulder and I shrieked.

Luther?...No, not even close.

A six-foot-tall, nothing-looking guy stood beside me. "Sorry, but

… uh … I think you're in my seat." He was so careful in his wording, as if talking to a time bomb. The way he dressed made me think of a Harvard professor—except his goatee and spiky hair made him look younger, like a student. He wore gray slacks instead of jeans, a button-down instead of a tee, and a tan blazer instead of a leather jacket like what the other patrons sported. Luther owned nothing as classy. Only jeans with holes, t-shirts covered with logos, and a ski jacket with overstuffed sleeves.

The stranger coughed politely and shrugged his brows. I got his point, but I couldn't speak. I tried to nod some kind of communication that said, *I can't move. Please take your stuff somewhere else.*

"Never mind," he conceded. "I'll just move over here."

He shuffled his books and notes, cramming them into his tan shoulder bag. The bag made a hideous thud as it landed on the nearest seat. The man stationed himself at the table to my left and stripped off his blazer quickly, as if the room had suddenly exploded with heat. He folded it over his arm, and then laid it behind his shoulder bag.

"Hey, Monica!" he called over his shoulder. "Mon, where's my corned beef?"

The waitress behind the bar rolled her eyes and tilted her head. "Aw, is the prince hungry?"

I casually turned around. Monica stood behind the bar flashing her braces and offering a royal bow. I wished my life were so simple that I could just stand behind a bar and joke with people—talk to people. Talk to anyone, even…

Would you just call him? …No, I can't talk to him. Not after all I said. "You don't really love me; you just think because you're my dad you can just RUN my life! I'm better off with Luther. He gets me."

I watched Monica as she bounced around behind the bar, cheerfully preparing a beverage. Then I turned to my neighbor, who had pulled out one stack of papers from his shoulder bag. He offered her another regal wave. She stuck out her tongue.

I miss having fun.

The Prince started laughing. He caught me looking in their direction and decided to fill me in on the joke. "My cousin's got a sense of humor, eh?"

I looked down at the table and quietly prayed that the heaviness in my groin would pass. I tried to discreetly fold my hands in my lap, lightly pushing between my legs—just in case my baby decided to pop out without warning.

Just don't let it happen yet. Please don't let it happen yet. Please.

Monica came out from behind the bar and stood next to The Prince. She looked my way but came no closer, as if I had some kind of contagious skin rash. "You, uh, you want something?" she asked.

"Water," I grunted. *Water and a miracle.*

The Prince elbowed her in the back as she shuffled away. "And my corned beef would be nice, too. Maybe with some extra chips."

I ignored her sarcastic reply. Through the window's white and green lettering, I watched a couple walk by with their arms around each other. They were young, maybe my age, and dressed in matching shades of blue. The man pulled his lady closer and nuzzled her hair. Maybe he was whispering something sweet. She curled into him and sighed. They made me feel ill.

Luther used to hold me like that—especially when he would tell me I looked hot.

I rubbed my belly. I wasn't so *hot* anymore. Greasy hair always up in a ponytail, fresh zits, and a body that now only fit in his old clothes. It was no wonder Luther had stopped holding me close.

Doesn't the fact that I'm carrying his kid mean anything?

I groaned. The Prince seemed to be trying to keep from looking my way. His lips fluttered for a second and his head bobbed like he wanted to speak.

Where's my water?

My right hand started rubbing my belly. I found myself whispering under my breath, "It's okay, Whitney…" This, unfortunately, triggered an invitation for him to speak.

"Is the baby kicking?" He leaned my way just a bit.

I nodded, opting to lie. *She's doing more than that. A lot more.*

"My sister just had one of those," he said, his hands mimicking the shape of a pregnant belly over his own flat stomach. "It was a boy. Looked like my uncle."

His head bobbed in the direction of Monica, who was back by the bar taking a phone call. I hoped he was referring to her father, not indicating that the waitress had recently undergone a sex change operation. He must have read my thoughts because he looked like he was ready to blush. He waved his hand to disconnect Monica from the discussion.

"Bald and pudgy," he clarified.

For some reason I pictured an elf stuffing his face with cookies and pie. "Your uncle's bald and pudgy."

The Prince smiled and pulled his gaze away like he was embarrassed. "Actually, no. But my nephew still reminds me of my uncle for some reason. Cute, though."

"Your uncle?" I didn't want to keep talking, but for some reason his smooth voice made me calm.

His grin widened. I saw more of his teeth. They were very white and straight. Not a single one had Luther's signature lightning bolt crack.

"Adam—my niece—nephew!" Obviously not a communications major. "My *nephew*, Adam." He mouthed the word "nephew" one more time. "It was supposed to be a girl," he explained. "*He*, I mean. He was supposed to be a girl." He smacked his lips. "They were expecting a girl, but … well, you know…"

His thought was lost. He pulled his shoulder back in, coiling back into his seat quietly.

Luther never asked if it was a boy or a girl. Not once. Not even when

I offered to tell him.

"So, it was a boy?" I asked. Forgetting about my discomfort for a moment, I started to enjoy his spacey babble. At least he was talking instead of leaving a note on the table saying he was sorry he couldn't keep his nephew's gender straight.

The Prince nodded. His head shot back to me quickly. "Yes, it's a boy. HE'S a boy." He exhaled heavily and turned his gaze to the front again. "They have to return a lot of gifts. I got him a dress and a little pink bear."

"Ya." I nodded with great certainty. "Those will have to go back."

"They were positive it was a girl. HE was a girl." He mouthed the word "girl" again.

Meanwhile, I pictured a short, bald man in a poofy pink dress—the kind bridesmaids often wear. I gave him a wide-rimmed hat like a southern belle and named him Clara. I smirked and let the image build, added music and made him do a little dance—a tap dance number.

Dance, Clara. Dance.

"He's cute, though, don't get me wrong. Tiny … just like…" He was making size assumptions with his hands, changing the distance between his palms several times as if he couldn't quite pull it out of memory. Six inches, then ten, then two, then fifteen.

"When was he born?" I asked to stop the measuring.

"Six hours ago." Finally, I saw the exhaustion in his eyes. The corners were deep red and the low light made the pouches under his lower lids look swollen. "St. Anthony's Hospital. Good place. Nurses were very nice…"

I hoped for the same, but I didn't know what I could expect at Denver General.

Monica swept by and left my water but no food for the Prince, who continued to rub his temples. Soon he started making a buzzing noise with his lips. Then he burst, "Thirty-six hours!"

I choked on my first sip. "Excuse me?"

"My sister... It took thirty-six hours," he clarified with a finger raised.

Not what I wanted to hear. My body started quivering again. *Luther, where are you? I need you here ... now!*

"I was there, though. I stood right there." He pointed to the floor as if he had given his support from the restaurant.

"Isn't that the dad's job?" His enthusiasm irritated me. Luther said once that when it came to "pushing the kid out," he would be waiting in the lobby or the nearest bar ... but he promised he'd have the crib assembled by Tuesday—any Tuesday.

"Adam's dad isn't around anymore." He rubbed his face with his hands and let out a low exhale.

This was a road I didn't want to go down. My body cramped. Baby was in motion. All of a sudden, I wanted help. I shifted and pushed against the seat of the chair. I was about to cry out ... but the discomfort shifted and my baby settled down.

"But, I did it." The Prince sat up proud like he couldn't see me cringing.

Oh, we're still on you? I nodded to avoid inciting more discussion. Whitney needed my focus, not him.

"I was there for thirty-six hours." He yawned. "Worth it, though... Just to see the little guy. Little Adam."

Thinking of that empty apartment and the note scattered down 8th Avenue, I asked, "Why did you do it? Wasn't your kid, so... I mean, thirty-six hours—"

"How could I not?" he interrupted. "She's my sister. There are certain things you just do for family."

Are there?

I turned my gaze solidly to the window. Playing back that message, *Britney, it's your father ... please ... just call me. I just need to know you're okay...* I started digging in my pocket for my cell phone.

What if there are?

The Prince spoke again, "This your first? An Adam?"

"A Whitney."

"You sure?"

I froze. *Question not kosher.*

He read my silence accurately. "Sorry … been a long day."

My long day was just beginning. I felt seriously uncomfortable again. I wanted to get up and move around, but my belly felt too heavy to carry.

"When are you due?"

I laughed to myself. I tried to come up with a clever response to mask my discomfort. A joke. A sarcastic remark. A weather report. Anything. Instead, I lunged forward, gripped the table surface, and gasped.

Damn him for speaking. HE SET IT OFF!

The Prince dove over to me, holding his blazer out. His expression said, *I got you.* I wanted to smack him and remind him that you can't catch thunder in a jacket. He saw the cell phone in my hand and took it.

"Is there someone I can call?" he asked.

I could think of only one person.

The Prince dialed and held the phone to my ear while I held my belly with both hands. There was a rush of pain and then a dripping sensation down my legs.

This is it!

I didn't start to cry until my father answered. Through my sobs, I tried to explain. I tried to put words together—words about Luther, about me, about the baby.

All he said was, "I'm coming to get you."

Rebecca Rowley, biographer of fictional characters, has been looking for her knight in shining publication since the age of seven. The Prince and Broken Water is chapter one of her publishing fairytale.

I Love Lucy
by Curtis Craddock

Jonah's battered Hummer rattled across the sun-baked scrubland of Ethiopia's highlands. A second-hand satellite radio on the passenger's seat hissed and popped, making the female announcer's smooth voice sound as rough and pockmarked as the old desert road.

"The authorities are still being closed-lipped about last week's break-in at the National Museum of Ethiopia in Addis Ababa. The curators have said only that one of the preservation rooms was broken into and that an inventory of all the artifacts is being conducted. This has led to speculation that the break-in may have had something to do with the skeletal remains of Australopithecus, a human ancestor—"

Jonah punched the radio off. "I did not derive from an ape." How could anyone let a bunch of hare-brained paleontologists—art school drops outs, the lot of them—tell him that life was an accident, that mankind had arrived here by way of muck? Who were they to say there were no souls? They perverted science.

Jonah was a particle physicist by trade and by training. He had looked into the subatomic world and seen the hand of God in interactions so tiny and so brief, they were barely more real than the mathematical equations that described them; and yet they supported the entire fabric of Creation. If matter was composed ultimately of information, and information could only exist in a matrix, then that matrix must be the mind of God, the same God who had made mankind in His own image, who had given humanity an iota of the divine.

The atheists, though, would never see the truth of God, no matter how plainly it was shown to them. They thought humans were nothing special, just another sort of animal without purpose or soul, so they made up evolution and rammed it down people's throats and called it science. Science was supposed to be neutral, supposed to be impartial, but something really objective couldn't contradict God.

The devil's greatest trick was convincing mankind that he doesn't exist.

Jonah kissed his fingertips and pressed them to a picture on the dashboard, the sun-faded image of a blonde woman with an angelic smile. His Molly. He missed her every waking moment and even in his dreams. She was the purest soul he'd ever met, kind, gentle, generous, and pious. Her faith in the sanctity of humanity's God-given soul had never wavered, not even in the face of a fatally complicated pregnancy … but the evilutionists wanted to take her soul away from her. He would not let them.

An instrument on the dashboard beeped and whined. The original sat-nav system had been ripped out and replaced with an arcane device with a tiny touch screen and a needle-like a compass under a glass bubble. The Frenchman had called it a *sympathomatograph*. He'd invented it to help find missing people. Just attach a little bit of that person to the leads of the device and it could point you straight to that person. Except the device didn't quite work as advertised. Instead of finding where a person was, the device found where they had been when the piece got separated from the original. Put in a hair from your missing daughter's brush and it would inevitably lead you to the bathroom where she'd brushed her hair out, where the skin tag on the follicle had died. As a search and rescue tool, the sympathomatograph had serious limits.

Jonah, however, had immediately seen its potential as an archeological tool. Insert the fossilized bone of, say, Australopithecus, and the sympathomatograph would take you to the place it died. Maybe you could find the rest of the skeleton. Maybe you could show people what a fraud the fossil really was, just like Piltdown man. Or maybe, with God's will, you could erase the cursed thing from history, if the evilutionist's didn't catch you up first.

Jonah checked his rear view mirror for the umpteenth time, but there was no sign of Sondra, Molly's sister, the red-headed nightmare of Jonah's life. She'd been after him for months, ever since his robbery at Stanford … as if it was any of her business. Yes, she had once been a federal agent, but these days she was just a civilian with a paleontology degree and a persistent nature. Yet she seemed to have the ear of every government official and military officer in a dozen countries, contacts from her earlier career. She was bound to be back there somewhere, chasing after him in a commandeered attack helicopter or something. And she had the nerve to tell him it was for his own good, as if he were an errant child

The sympathomatograph's slowly oscillating needle quivered and began to spin in circles. Jonah's pulse quickened; he had arrived. By the time he finished unloading his equipment from the Hummer, night fell and chill air replaced the blistering heat of the sun.

He set up the generators, the computers, the arc generator, the singularity web, the quantum disruptor. Truly his project was an international effort. He'd begged, borrowed and even stolen components from all over the globe, from narrow-minded scientists who had no idea about the potential of their inventions. It was God's will that guided Jonah and let him see what these devices were meant to be used for.

The snake-oil pseudo-science of evolution was about to be cut off at the knees. Sondra would be too late. Indeed, no one would ever be more too late than she. By the time Sondra arrived, he would have erased, not the evidence of a crime, but the crime itself.

By midnight he was ready, and exhausted. Sondra was nowhere in sight. No helicopters buzzed along the cliff tops, no Hummers bounced up the road after him. Thank God.

He fired up his computers and uplinked them via satellite to a battery of the world's most powerful supercomputers. Then he shrugged into the singularity web's harness.

The Russian he'd bought the rig from had tried to explain the principle of the device's operation to him. "You can't go back in time," he'd said, "because the past isn't there anymore. It spreads out like an explosion and gets absorbed into all the subsequent instants."

But you can recreate *the past.*

Take a bomb and blow it up. Bits and pieces fly in every direction, but if you can record the vector, velocity, and spin of enough fragments, you can build an accurate picture of the moment of detonation. Now imagine, the Russian had said, if you could do the same thing with time. Capture enough basic particles, calculate them backwards, and you could get an accurate picture of a moment in time, assuming you could calculate the coordinates properly. He'd built a device to do just that, and Jonah had purchased it from him.

A Japanese physicist had supplied the final piece of the puzzle. If time was elementary, as the flat shape of the quantum universe suggested, then wormholes didn't exist naturally, but there was nothing to stop someone with the right sort of equipment from creating spikes in space-time. An ambitious man could use these worm-cul-de-sacs to insert data into the quantum constructs of the past-time generator— and *change* the past.

The arc generator hummed as it came up to power. Jonah attached the output leads from the sympathomatograph to his computer and watched the hourglass on the screen as dozens of linked machines spun through unfathomable amounts of data.

For more than an hour, the space-time program crunched numbers. Jonah fidgeted. The go-pill made him edgy. He checked and double-checked his traveling equipment, the stealth suit, the camera, the experimental, man-portable laser gun. Light was the universal solvent on the quantum level, energy that was its own medium, and the only thing that could reach through the temporal matrix and redirect the energy flow of the past … he hoped. If he was wrong, if his calculations were off, he might perform the world's greatest vanishing act. Not even the memory of him would be left.

Nervous and agitated, he paced the perimeter of his lantern light, peering into the surrounding dark through an infrared imager. Every now and then, he imagined movement out there on the barren scarp, but he heard no engine noise and the imager showed no white-hot engine signatures, just the deep-red, lumpy, indistinct forms of a few large animals trudging about on whatever nightly business large animals had. Were there any lions left in Ethiopia, or had the poachers got them all? He'd never bothered to find out. Lions weren't important. He fondled his pistol in its holster for comfort.

He gave up pacing and sought refuge in his Bible, the one Molly had given him on the day he'd been born again. She escorted him to the altar with a giddy glee that presaged their marriage, and he accepted Christ as his savior and all his sins had been washed away.

The Good Book read, *Then God said, "Let us make man in our image, after our likeness; and let them have dominion over the fish of the sea, and over the birds of the air, and over the cattle, and over all the earth, and over every creeping thing that creeps upon the earth." So God created man in his own image, in the image of God he created him; male and female he created them.*

God created man. You couldn't get any more clear than that. He had made men separate from animals. He had made them in His own image—not His own physical image, obviously, because God had no physical image, but rather in His spiritual image. He had given men souls. To say men came up from apes and apes came up from mud was to therefore deny God.

Molly had known better.

The computer beeped, and the display lit up with a green go-ahead sign. And now the moment of truth. He made his way to the arc generator, took a knee, and prayed, "O Father, who art in Heaven, hallowed be thy name. Dear Lord, I ask you to give me the strength to endure my trials and to overcome your enemies. Help me to undo the lies that your deniers have spread, so that all may experience your righteous glory. Forgive the sinners, for they know not what they do—"

"What we do, Jonah, is arrest crazy buggers like you for theft, smuggling and espionage." A woman's sharp voice.

Jonah whirled and found himself face to face with Sondra, a six-foot, lanky red-head with eyes like chips of diamond. Jonah met her gaze, so self-assured, so angry. Atheists were always angry. The demons inside them kept them mad to prevent them from feeling God's grace and accepting His truth.

She and half a dozen Ethiopian soldiers fanned out around him, guns drawn. He almost asked how they sneaked up on him, but behind them were horses ... large, lumpy animals moving quietly in the dark.

Sondra said, "Hands up, Jonah. This show is over." Her voice softened. "And you need help. For Molly's sake, don't make me hurt you."

Jonah bristled from the very base of his spine. "This *is* for Molly's sake."

"Do you really think she would have wanted you to commit grand theft?"

Jonah smiled a brittle smile. "She wanted me to minister to the world." He pressed the activation button on his harness.

"Oh, shit!" Sondra lunged for him.

Time went very ... strange. It did not so much rewind as implode, each instant collapsing in on the one before. Deafening flashes of smell blinded his skin. It lasted a moment. It lasted forever.

Jonah stood in a field of tall grass. A warm breeze caressed his face. The sun beat down on a lush savannah of bluish grass interspersed with islands of strange trees that hadn't been there a moment ... ago. Except a moment ago was the future. If all the technology had worked correctly, he should be back before the Flood, very nearly to the time of the Fall, almost four thousand years before Christ.

His arrival had not gone unnoticed. Far across the field, a herd of animals looked in his direction. They were like horses, or maybe zebras, only smaller, with rough manes and black stripes on tawny bodies.

Closer by, nearly hidden in the grass, was a group of monkeys, except not monkeys.

They had brownish fur more sparse than a chimpanzee's, and flatter faces, and they walked on two legs. *Australopithecus!*

Jonah's heart raced. Blood pounded in his ears, and it was all he could do to breathe quietly, though they shouldn't be able to hear him. Only fundamental light, the first thing God created, could cross the quantum barrier. Johan found it rather like watching a silent movie without the ambient whirr of a projector. The creatures should not be able to see him in his sneak suit—designed to break up his outline and blend him into the background—but they all peered in his direction

Yes, they bore a superficial resemblance to humans. He could see how an eager, imaginative mind, duped by Darwin, might see their skulls and think them somehow related to man, but to see them alive was a totally different animal. Their shiny black eyes held no native intelligence, no God-given spark of rational thought or soul. They were just another unfortunate species of ape that hadn't survived the Flood. Noah had saved every *kind* of animal—some felines, some canines, some bovines—not every *species.*

From behind him came a flicker and a groan. The almost-zebras bolted for the cover of trees. The Australopithecines scattered. Jonah whirled to find Sondra, or at least the translucent ghost of Sondra, suspended in the air behind him. She was spread-eagled, her limbs outstretched to their fullest, as if she clung to the side of a giant invisible beach ball.

She had charged him just as he activated the quantum disruptor, and she … she must have been caught in the singularity web. Now she was stuck there like an impurity on the face of a soap bubble.

"Oh, God," she whimpered. "Help." Her form shimmered and buzzed.

"So now you believe," Jonah said. In moments of extreme duress, even His most strident doubters called His name. What surer proof could there be of His presence?

"Figure of speech," she grunted, focusing on him even as she turned away from Grace once more. "What the hell did you do to me?"

"We've come back in time."

"Time? What, how?"

"In a quantum bubble." He resisted the urge to explain the math to her; he didn't have the time and she wouldn't understand. "You got caught on the fringe."

"Jesus, bloody hell." She fizzed and sparked. A sudden uncertainty gnawed at Jonah's heart. He hadn't intended to bring her here, and he had no idea what would happen to her when the quantum bubble popped. Would she return to the future, or would she evaporate in a quantum spray of elementary particles? Surely whatever happened to her was her own fault for getting in the way. But that did not mean he wanted to be part of anyone's death, especially his sister-in-law's. Molly would hate that; she had loved Sondra in spite of her sins. Yet only God could help Sondra now, but she had to believe. Perhaps if he could loosen materialism's death grip on her brain, she could be made to see the reality of Heaven.

He returned his attention to the space where the Australopithecus had been lurking, but all the beasts were gone—except one. A simian face stared in his direction through the tall grass, its eyes curious. It must be able to see Sondra trapped like a spider in a web of her own meddling. It was a smaller creature, young or female, legs too long and arms too short to be a chimp, but definitely not human, nor anything that would ever become human. Would Sondra see that? Evolutionists were notorious for seeing only the evidence they wanted to see. Still, he had to try, for Molly's sake and the sake of Sondra's soul.

"I've found something you might want to see." Jonah stepped aside and gestured toward the creature.

Sondra's gaze followed his direction. Her eyes took a moment to focus, but then she gasped, "Lucy!"

"As you can see, it's just an animal, an ape, not a human."

Her own pain apparently forgotten, Sondra said, "She's beautiful. Look at the way she holds her shoulders, square, not rounded, and her thumbs and her feet ... Oh, no. She's trapped."

Jonah looked closer at the ape. Indeed, its foot was trapped between an up-thrust rock and a fallen log. Was this how the fossil called Lucy died? Trapped and unable to free itself until some predator happened along to scatter its bones? With the fossil as its anchor point, the quantum bubble should have arrived very near the time and place of the creature's death, plus or minus the load of an unexpected passenger. And what was Sondra's presence doing to the integrity of the bubble? It would certainly be an extra power bleed, so he didn't have much time.

A course of action suggested itself. He powered up his laser gun. Fundamental light could breach the quantum gap. He took aim.

"Stop!" Sondra cried. "What are you doing?"

"Witnessing," he said.

"By shooting an innocent? Is that what Molly would have wanted?"

Jonah's heart bled every time Sondra spoke his wife's name. He said, "You never understood her. You tried to have her committed."

"Because choosing to die rather than ending an ectopic pregnancy is not a rational decision."

Jonah rounded on her. "The child had a soul! To abort it would have been murder."

"And to keep it was suicide, which is also a mortal sin. Pick one."

Jonah's jerked the laser around to point at Sondra. Not that he would fire ... even if he knew what it would do to her. "She died protecting my child. That is not suicide."

Sondra stared past the muzzle of the weapon. "But how does that bring us here? Killing Lucy wont bring Molly back."

Jonah shook his head. "You don't understand. Molly is in a better place. She earned her spot in Heaven, but she left me behind to spread His word." He returned his aim to the Australopithecus and keyed off the safety. He would change the data. All the quanta that had been reconstructed here would explode outward in a new pattern, a new future.

"Is your God a butcher?" Sondra spat, squirming on the surface of the bubble.

"No." Jonah fired. The primordial laser struck the branch that pinned the ape's foot. The branch scorched and severed. The Australopithecus screeched and leapt away, scurrying into the tall grass. Jonah let out a breath as long-held tension unwound in his chest. "He is merciful."

Sondra's eyes crossed in her perplexity. "I don't get it."

Now that the deed was done, a welcome calm stole over Jonah. It was his job to witness. "Gullible men, tempted by Satan or their own pride, find these bones and delude themselves into thinking they are our ancestors, men from apes, from microorganisms, from mud, but that is not what the Bible says—"

"The Bible is a parable!"

"The Bible says man has a soul. Mud has no soul. It is impossible for a soul to evolve from nothing, but people like you can't see that."

"It's not even a scientific question," Sondra protested.

"Because the so-called science of evolution asks only questions that cannot be answered by God." He shook his head. "But people have to made to see. Mankind is special, made in God's image."

Sondra's voice whined in distortion and pain. "I think I understand. You think that if science is correct and humankind arose by evolution, then we have no souls ... which means that Molly died for nothing."

Jonah's teeth gnashed. "She. Did. Not!" He took a moment to gather himself, to focus on the matter at hand. "God's truth is the Truth. It must be told, but I have no gift for oratory, no great wealth or influence, so I have found a way to reveal the Truth scientifically, by obliterating the lies that obscure it.

"Fossils are very rare things, products of innumerable unlikely coincidences. An animal has to die in exactly the right, very rare circumstances. If the creature"—he waved generally behind him— "didn't die here, then its bones will not be scattered here, and it will never be dug up here.

"All of the so-called ancestral bones of mankind ever found, including this Australopithecus, would, if gathered in one place, fit quite comfortably in a rain barrel. It will not be hard for me to track them down, to alter history so they are never fossilized and never found. And if there are no missing links, no celebrity skeletons, the lie of man's evolution will have no hold over gullible imaginations. Other animals may have evolved, but mankind will remain as God intended us to be: special, moral, spiritual."

"You don't like the conclusion so you destroy the evidence," Sondra said. "Is that what you think Molly would have wanted? Besides, there will still be plenty of evidence for evolution, even for man's. There is DNA and—"

"The rest is just drawings and numbers and things people can't see. Yes, the atheist fringe will still worship Darwin the monkey god, but regular honest, hard-working, God-fearing people will not be tempted into lies. Molly would have liked that. She put her faith before everything."

Sondra's face went very still as it so often did when a realization struck her. "She even put it before you. It was more important to her than you were. She dumped you for God, and you're still trying to prove yourself worthy of her. The rest is just wind."

Jonah's anger flared. "Shut up! Molly loved me, but she wasn't willing to kill our child to save her own life."

"Because the child had a soul," Sondra said calmly, despite the feedback whine. Her body was fading, becoming more translucent by the moment. Was she being pulled back to the future-present, or was she dissolving into the quantum void?

She said, "Tell me, Jonah. How can you tell if someone is ensouled?"

The question caught Jonah by surprise. "Because the Bible says they are."

"But surely you ought to be able to confirm that hypothesis. What do people do that is evidence they have souls? Is it acts of charity, or rituals to unseen forces, or prayer?"

"All of those things," Jonah said warily. "And sacrifice."

"Then I suggest you look behind you," she said in a voice barely more than an echo.

Jonah turned. The ape had returned. He could tell it was the same one by the abrasion on its leg. In its arms, it bore bunches of a strange purple fruit that it placed deliberately on the ground, in a straight line between itself and Jonah, almost like ... an offering.

The Australopithecus got down on its stubby knees and spread its arms wide in a gesture of supplication. It raised its face to the sky and let out what he imagined was a long ululating cry. After a moment, more of the monkeys emerged from the brush. And each of them laid a fruit on the ground next to the first. Then they took to their knees and raised their arms and began to chant.

"Congratulations," Sondra said. "You've just become a god." And then she was gone.

For a long moment, Jonah stood and stared unblinking and unthinking at the spectacle before him. This was impossible. Animals didn't ... they couldn't ... but these did. They gave food and they gave thanks. They conceived of a world of unseen forces. They weren't human, but they were ... people.

"God help me," he whispered, and the quantum bubble popped.

#

Sound returned in a rush. The chatter of voices and the hum of machinery yanked on his attention, but Jonah kept his eyes squeezed shut, trying to hang onto the memory of the moment. He knew his mission had failed. If he had succeeded in erasing Lucy from humanity's consciousness, then the Awash Valley would be just another bit of lonely desert, and there would have been no reason for Sondra to chase him here. There wouldn't be any noise.

Instead, any second now, the soldiers would seize him and pin his arms and clap him in handcuffs and drag him off to be drawn and quartered between a dozen nation states. Yet, just now, he couldn't bring himself to be too disappointed. The Australopithecines were not men, maybe not even men's ancestors, but people with souls. Would they not be treasured by God?

"Hey, Jonah!" Sondra's hand landed on his shoulder even as her voice penetrated his awareness. "Time to wake up."

Jonah sighed and opened his eyes to a tableau every bit as unexpected as the antediluvian veldt. Instead of soldiers, his camp was surrounded by men and women dressed in the eclectic style of archaeologists, somewhere between beach bum and Indiana Jones. Half a dozen news crews in stylish safari gear lingered around a large circus-type tent behind a press line.

He blinked uncertainly and stared up into Sondra's eyes. "You're alive!"

"Yes," she said. "And I'm apparently one of only two people who remember how this whole mess got started. In fact, I seem to have two sets of memories about the whole thing. One in which you are a criminal nutter fleeing through Ethiopia with half a billion in stolen technical equipment, and another in which you are a respected scientist unveiling a new archaeological tool, a time viewer. The conflict between these views is … disconcerting."

Jonah's mind grasped the technical problem as the easier to deal with. "It must be because you were trapped in the fringe of the quantum bubble. I only have one set of memories. The criminal one."

"So you don't know how you've changed things. Hah!"

"I … I am sorry." And he was. "I didn't understand. I still don't."

"Good. That means you're starting to think like a scientist again. As it turns out, your plan backfired rather spectacularly. After your rescue, Lucy's tribe apparently decided this spot was sacred, so instead of finding a few scattered bones, science uncovered a dozen mostly intact skeletons arranged in such a way as to suggest a ritualized burial. In other words, culture."

Jonah's mind tried to take this in, but it seemed to have reached a saturation point. The questions of Lucy's soul, of God's plan, were too big to handle all at once, so he reached out for the only other thing that mattered. "Molly?" If the world had changed so much, might not she have chosen differently this time around?

Sondra grimaced. "She always was stubborn. She would rather die than doubt."

"She wouldn't see it that way. She would say she would rather die than betray a truth."

"And you? You said you wanted to witness to the world. Well, the world is here." She gestured to the camera crews. "What are you going to tell them?"

Jonah stared unseeing at the media people. It was a sin to bear false witness, but what was true? He used to be certain, but that creature, Australopithecus, Lucy, had an awareness of forces beyond her comprehension. She showed thanks and reverence. She had a soul.

Could humankind have come from that? Could the shaping of humanity from dust really have gone through a process of stages and transitional forms? It no longer seemed so inconceivable. What if the question of evolution wasn't so much the "if" but the "how" of God's creation? God was not the numbers on the dice, or the odds of the throw, or the result of the toss. He was the subtle weaver, the unquantifiable chance that slid between the smallest possible moments and guided the outcome. He worked in mysterious ways, but every now and then, He tipped his hand.

Jonah pulled the picture of Molly from his pocket and stared into her angelic eyes, and suddenly the reason for her death was unimportant. The only thing that mattered was her absence, and the hole it left inside him that anger and frustration could not fill. There was only one way to honor her, and that was to plant a seed of wonder in that hole and sprinkle it with curiosity, and take joy in whatever new life sprouted up.

"You say it was a graveyard?" he asked, stumbling into a new and fascinating uncertainty.

"Complete with funerary artifacts. They've found fossilized pollen, which indicates flowers were buried with the dead, and, well, a lot more." With obvious effort, she restrained herself from further explanation.

"Flowers." Jonah shook his head in wonderment. "I ... I think..." He stared in the direction of the camera crews. People were going to expect him to talk. The whole world would be watching. "I think I must bear witness to their souls."

Curtis Craddock is a writer and illustrator who earns his bread as a teacher in a state prison out in the twilight zone. His first novel, a dark fantasy called Sparrow's Flight, *was published in 2000. He is currently working on his master's degree.*

Devastation Mine
by Nikki Baird

Sam stood on the back balcony of his mountain house and surveyed the valley below. He knew pine beetles had overrun the hills nearby, but this was the first time he'd seen how badly.

For fifteen years, since he and his wife had first found this lovely refuge from demanding careers, Sam had stood on this balcony to stare into the dark mystery of the trees below. They had marched up the hill all the way to the back of the house, and he had loved every tree. No matter the arguments or all-out fights that might have occurred inside as his marriage fell apart, he could always find peace in the view out back.

Looking at it now, all he saw was devastation. Sometime over the summer, Forest Service personnel had stripped the hillside bare, all the way down into the valley below and partway up the other side. A vast forest had been reduced to a rocky wasteland littered with the wreckage of trees. In some places, not even stumps marked the ravaged land. Machines had left giant tread marks behind, scraping the land raw. Only a few trees remained, a stray fir or spruce, and a stand of aspen trees far off to the south.

Karen sighed as she stepped onto the back balcony, shoulder to shoulder with him. "Can you believe what they've done?" she said.

So many dead trees posed an enormous fire hazard. But that didn't make Sam feel any better. "This is one of the saddest things I think I've ever seen," he whispered.

"I think so too," Karen answered. She gathered his hand in hers, a touch he had not felt in a long time.

Sam managed to stop himself from jerking away in surprise. It was the first time they had shared a moment that wasn't an acid exchange of bitter, hurt feelings since the divorce was finalized. He stood next to her for a long moment, trying to get used to the new, impersonal feeling of his ex-wife's hand in his, as his eyes adjusted to the newly bare view.

Long-familiar landmarks were now gone. Like their marriage, Sam couldn't help thinking. Faced with the destruction wrought by the divorce, it was hard to recognize the landmarks of even the highest points of their twenty-five-year marriage—including many memories created in this very house.

But that, too, was about to be stripped bare, as they spent the day dividing up the last of their shared possessions so the house could be sold. Another fond memory chewed up and spat out. Sam grimaced.

A flash of light caught his eye, sunlight on metal. He glanced to his left, leaning out over the balcony as he looked for the source. It winked again in the mid-day light. "What's that?" He pointed.

Karen shaded her eyes with her hand and followed the direction he indicated. "I don't see anything," she said. "Oh, wait! That flash? Is that what you mean?"

"Yeah." Sam leaned even farther, trying to make out details. It was far off to the left, southeast of the house, where the lonely stand of aspen trees shimmered a brilliant yellow against the fall sky. "I don't think we ever went very far that way."

"No, the trees just got too thick."

Seized by a sudden impulse, Sam turned to her. "Let's go check it out."

Karen frowned. "It's probably glass from something one of the Forest Service guys dropped."

"C'mon, Kare, this'll be our last chance to see what's over there," he wheedled. "We've been working on packing the house up all morning—let's take a break and check it out. Tell me you're not just a little curious..."

"Oh, all right," she relented. "Let me get my coat." She sounded exasperated, but Sam caught the excited look on her face as she headed inside. He felt it too. He didn't know why, but he wanted to walk the land one more time—*their* land, that they had both worked so hard to get.

So hard, we forgot to work on the marriage, Sam thought, seized for the first time not by anger but by regret.

It took nearly an hour to reach the spot where something twinkled in the bright afternoon sunlight. They both puffed from navigating the desolate landscape as they approached it.

"Is it a piece of metal?" Karen panted as they came within yards of the item.

Sam lunged up the hill, his long legs carrying him quickly to the spot. He could feel Karen's eyes on him as he bent down to inspect it. A twist of railroad track gleamed in the sun. As soon as he realized what it was, he straightened quickly, excitement vibrating through him as he peered into the stand of aspen trees.

"Come look at this!" He beckoned to her, grinning like a child. "You're not going to believe it!"

Karen thrust her hands in her pockets and strode up the hill.

"Look," he breathed, pointing to the twist of rusty metal. The Forest Service logging machines had just skimmed a piece of old railroad track, probably catching the edge in a tractor or backhoe tread long enough to scrape off a thick layer of rust and turn the piece upward *just so*—so the sun might catch it as someone looked out over the valley on a crisp, clear autumn day.

Sam pointed along the track's path. It curved slightly past the aspen, disappearing around a fold in the hill. Other than the one shiny piece, the track was in bad shape. The rotted remains of railroad ties marched into the aspens. Nails had rusted away completely in places, setting the rails free to wander drunkenly along the ties.

Sam glanced a question back at Karen, boyish excitement lifting the last few years from his shoulders. She grinned back and nodded. Together they followed the track.

"It's too narrow to be a railroad track," Sam commented as they hurried alongside it. "I think it was for an ore car."

"A mining claim, you think?"

Sam nodded.

A little ravine appeared before them, making a cut into the hillside. The track led straight inside. Their steps slowed as they eyed the gap in the hill. Silence descended over them, broken only by the scattered rattle of leaves in the aspens as a gust of wind whistled overhead.

Just past a dogleg bend, a small clearing came into view. Dead center in the back wall of the ravine, the square opening of an old mine shaft gaped at them. The railroad tracks proceeded straight into the mine. An old pile of tailings sprouted weeds and small trees off to the left, testimony to the site's original purpose. To the right, a one-room, windowless log cabin slumped into a slowly settling pile of lumber.

Oppressive silence descended on them both as they edged further into the little clearing. Karen shuddered, pulling her jacket tighter.

"Can you believe this was here the whole time and we never found it?" she marveled, her voice low as she surveyed the entire site.

Sam nodded agreement, cautiously approaching the entrance to the mine. The opening exhaled cold, dank air, prickling the hair on the back of his neck.

"You're not going in there, are you?" Karen gasped.

Sam reached out and touched the closest support beam at the mine's mouth. It crumbled at his touch. He turned back to Karen, a rueful grin on his lips. "No, I guess not."

They both turned to the cabin. Goosebumps crawled down Sam's arms, as if a cold presence lurked just beyond the rough-hewn door. Karen shuddered again.

Sam saw it and quirked his eye at her, stifling his own chill. "Want to try that?" he asked, challenging her a little. It would irritate her that he made it a challenge—it was almost force of habit that made him bait her.

She rubbed at her shoulders. "No harm in looking."

She waited until he reached her side so they could push the door open together. Sam nearly expected someone to be standing inside, and jumped himself when Karen spooked as the door scraped an agonizing trail across the dirt floor. It echoed through the clearing.

A stale cinnamon smell wafted out to them. Karen wrinkled her nose. "What is that?"

"Dunno." Sam shoved the door farther into the building. The whole thing creaked and shivered, but held. A faint square of light fell onto the bare, hard-packed floor. Rusty tin cans were just visible beyond the light, and darker shapes suggested furniture deeper in. Sam turned to Karen. "What do you think?"

Karen hesitated, and for a moment Sam thought she would go back. It was a creepy little shack, and he was suddenly more than willing to leave, now they had peeked inside.

Instead, Karen shrugged, surprising him. "We've come this far." And with that, she took a breath and strode boldly inside, ducking her head under the door's sagging frame.

Sam followed a step behind her, carefully edging the door as wide as it would go to let in more light. As their eyes adjusted, it became clear that whoever had been here last had left in a hurry. Belongings scattered in every direction—a tin plate lay here, rusty cans of food there, their labels peeling and unreadable. A thick layer of dust coated everything, including the remains of a bed to the left, a small cast iron oven in the back right corner, and an overturned pine table in the middle of the room. Karen craned her neck to peer beyond the table and gasped, her hands covering her mouth.

"What is it?" Sam followed her gaze. A chill ran down his spine when he realized what she found.

Two bodies lay intertwined, decayed to near skeletons, but still remarkably well preserved by the dry Colorado air. Long wisps of hair and other debris Sam didn't care to dwell on piled around the bodies. Between that and the desiccated remains of clothing, he gathered that the two were man and woman, either husband and wife or brother and sister, from the way they clasped each other.

The air, close and still since they had stepped into the clearing, began to stir through the ravine. Even from inside the cabin, the two of them heard it gusting through the trees, first shaking leaves, then stirring branches. As Sam and Karen turned to look, the swirl of wind blew into the cabin with enough force to raise the dust around them and rattle the tins on the floor.

Karen exclaimed in disgust, her hands clamped over her mouth. She and Sam both lunged for the door, squinting their eyes against the flying debris as the wind stiffened against them. One more powerful swirl through the cabin interior and the door slammed shut just as they reached it. It wouldn't budge. The cabin shuddered in protest.

Dust hung thick in the sudden stillness. Gaps around the ill-fitting door and holes in the crumbling chinking between the logs cast faint spears of light onto the powdery air. The ground rumbled beneath their feet, echoed by the creaking cabin.

Sam grabbed Karen's arm and pulled her to him. She grasped him back, coughing.

"What's happening?" she wailed.

"I don't know," he said, groping with one hand for the door handle.

Dim light flickered in the middle of the room, coalescing into the form of a woman. Her image jittered and bounced, like a poorly preserved film on an old movie projector. The dust swirled through her, creating an impromptu screen for her projection. She moved about, her hands motioning with unknown purpose. The objects she held had not been captured by whatever had maintained her image.

Karen clutched at Sam's arm. "What is that?" she whispered.

Sam put a reassuring hand over hers and drew her close, though his own heart hammered in his chest.

The woman before them wore layers and layers of clothing, wools and knits over muslin skirts. The long braid down her back might once have been tight and neat but now had chunks pulled out in places, as if she had been in a struggle. As they stared at her in wonder, frozen in fear, Sam found himself amazed at the detail of the image. He could see her breath puff in the air, even though the early fall day wasn't nearly that chill.

The stuttering image seemed oblivious to their presence. The woman fussed about with something they couldn't see—something that would have sat on the table had that been upright in the room. Sam's imagination filled in the missing pieces of the action. When she turned to add something to a bundle of clothing on the bed—the crumbling bundle still sat there—Sam saw tear tracks smeared through the dirt on her face. Her hands shook.

A second flickering form resolved into the shape of a man directly in front them, blocking the door. Sam yanked Karen to the right, keeping them both clear of the eerie scene.

Ye're not leavin', Missy! the man yelled, his fists balled at his sides and his face ruddy with anger. The words pressed into Sam's head, a thick Irish brogue, and from the way Karen stiffened in his arms, he knew she heard it, too.

Missy's ghostly form whirled to face the man. *I'm not doin' this no more!* she screeched back in a rolling Southern accent. *We's out of food, Cal. There's barely enough to get us to Georgetown!* She shoved bundles on the bed into a knapsack and yanked the strings shut. *I'm leavin', and if there's any sense left in that thick head a yours, you'll come too.* She held her head down as she faced him, like a bull ready to charge.

Cal immediately became softer with her. *Please, Missy. I can't run this all by meself.* He crossed the room, put his arms on her shoulders and squeezed gently.

Tears streamed down her face. *I can't,* she whispered, and brushed past him to grab something off the table.

Ye faithless bitch! Cal bellowed. He paced in front of the bed, angry all over again. *I know it's there. Just a little further...* He looked up at her, obsession and a little madness snapping in his eyes. *Will ye go back to the hard scrabble in Denver? Will ye beg on the street then?* He grabbed her arm again. *We can make it here—make something that's OURS!* He half-pleaded, half-threatened her.

Missy yanked her arm back, stumbling against the table. It rocked with her weight. *I can't do this, Cal. I won't.* She wouldn't meet his eyes.

Cal barricaded the door with his body, his arms thrown wide. His voice rumbled, low and dangerous. *Ye're not leavin' and you're sure as hell not takin' the food, neither.*

I can't make it t' town without it! Missy grabbed a knife off the table, pointed it at Cal, and grated, *If you want to die, that's your business. Get out of my way.*

Put that knife down! Cal roared as he lunged for her. Missy swung wildly with the knife as they came together. They broke apart, Missy banging into the table. Cal stumbled backward into the wall. Missy held the knife up with a shaking hand. It was slick with blood.

Sam sucked in his breath, shocked to feel an answering flash of pain in his side. It grew into a burning fire in his gut. Karen glanced a mute question at him, terror plain on her face. Sam lifted one shaking hand to his stomach but ignored Karen when she tugged urgently at his arm. Cal and Missy held him rapt, his head swimming and his heart bathed in icy fear. What happened next suddenly became the most important thing in the whole world.

Cal began to slide to the floor, clutching at his stomach.

Missy screamed, shaking her head in denial before flinging the knife aside. She looked from Cal to the packs on the bed and table, torn. She tightened her lips, her face pale, and began to gather up her things once more.

Bitch! he gasped at her from the floor. *Would ye leave me here to die?* Missy refused to answer. Tears ran down her face.

Cal reached over his head and with a fumbling tug, pulled his rifle from its peg by the door. Slow, laborious movements got the gun wedged onto his knee, where he could aim it at Missy. He grunted in triumph.

She turned at the sound. Her eyes widened in shock as she tried to mouth a denial. Cal's hand rocked backwards as he pulled the trigger and Missy spasmed, tumbling over the table and knocking it over.

Karen shrieked. Sam knew it was coming—had known something like this would happen from the moment he felt the echo of Missy's knife in his own gut. He managed to catch Karen before she collapsed to the floor, but the effort sent him to his knees. The room began to spin around him.

Cal cried out, regretful. He stumbled around the upset table. Reaching Missy, he gathered her in his arms, both of them crying.

I didn't mean it, she whispered, reaching up to touch his face.

Shhh, Cal admonished. *I didn't mean it neither._*

Missy's eyes fluttered shut and Cal howled his grief, bending his head over hers.

Sam clutched at Karen, fearful that the powerful echoes of these deaths were strong enough to sweep the two of them up with it. Fright constricted his heart until the apparitions faded away into the skeletal remains still frozen in grief.

A creeping blackness tried to claim Sam's vision and he fought it off, sure that his and Karen's lives depended on it. He pulled Karen's still form toward the door, gasping from the effort and the pain in his stomach.

Missy's image reappeared in the center of the room. She began frantically assembling her scant belongings. Sam's pain and dizziness passed at once, almost stunning in their absence.

He did not wait another instant. He hitched his arms around Karen's waist and dragged her to the door. It resisted his rough handling, but finally opened just as Cal reappeared to argue with Missy once again.

Sam managed ten feet before he collapsed in the clearing. He leaned his head back on the ground, grateful for the fall sunlight. Karen began to stir in his arms, and he pulled her close.

They clung to each other for a moment, gasping. Karen pulled away first.

"Are you hurt?" she asked, pressing her hands to his chest and stomach.

Sam shook his head. He covered her hands with his own, stilling her frantic attempts to find a wound. "No more than you—right?" He peered up into her eyes, concern for her that he had not felt in years chasing around his heart.

Karen eased out of his grip and settled next to him on the ground. "I'm okay." She rubbed self-consciously at her chest. "I don't want to feel that again, though."

"No." Sam glanced up at the cabin. "I wonder what would've happened if we didn't escape?"

"I don't know," she answered, "but we can't leave them like that." Her voice still shook. "It's like they're stuck. Forever."

Sam nodded, thinking of Cal, obsessed with his claim. How both he and Missy, even as the argument grew beyond either's control, still loved each other through their worst moment. Sam wondered suddenly if a happy couple would have seen what Karen and he saw.

"Sam!" Karen tugged at his coat.

He shook her off, noting the distress in her voice. "Yeah. Yeah. But what should we do?"

"I think we need to burn them," Karen whispered. "Burn their bones."

Sam looked down at her, startled. "How could you know that?"

Karen shrugged. "I saw a movie."

Sam glanced over at the cabin and the relative lack of vegetation in the ravine. Fall was a dangerous time to start a fire, but he couldn't deny the idea felt right. Then he shook his head. "I don't have a light."

"I do." Karen sounded surprised. She reached into her jeans pocket and pulled out the Zippo lighter they usually kept in the junk drawer back at the house. She held it out in a trembling hand and laughed at herself. "I don't really know why I wanted it," she said, running her thumb over the smooth surface. "And I didn't want to argue about it."

She held it out to Sam, a sheepish smile lingering on her face. "You can have it, if you want it. Somehow, I don't really care anymore." She glanced over at the cabin, shuddering. "But you're going to have to set the fire. I don't think I can go in there again."

Sam clasped his hand over hers and squeezed gently before lifting the heavy metal lighter out of her palm. He had been looking for it when they started sorting through the kitchen this morning, but like Karen, he suddenly didn't care what happened to it anymore. He nodded at her, and after a moment's hesitation, she nodded back.

Sam ducked into the cabin, and in no time at all emerged, the lighter conspicuously missing. After only a few minutes more, smoke began billowing out through the doorway. They stood together in silence and watched the cabin burn.

"We're lucky, aren't we?" she asked as the flames peaked. "For all the hurt between us, it never got this bad."

Sam barked out a startled laugh. "No," he agreed. "We never tried to kill each other, thank God." But he knew what she meant. "No," he repeated, thoughtful. "It never did." He smiled, a small, sad smile. "We had something good, didn't we? While it lasted?"

Karen nodded. Sam caught her hand a moment and squeezed before letting go. She smiled back at him. The distance was still there—too much had happened to undo that now. But forgiveness, something new, lay fresh between them.

They stood there until the cabin burned to ash.

Nikki Baird

When Nikki Baird is not writing fiction, she is speaking and writing about trends in retail technology. Her background runs from degrees in business, international politics, Russian, and physics, with a love for everything science fiction and supernatural. This is her first short story.

Opportunity Howls
by Barb A. Smith

I squinted at the weathered numbers on the log building through the windshield and checked my notes for the third time.

Damn. This was the right address.

I clunked my head against the steering wheel. My chest clutched with despondency. Who would want to meet way out here? Either I wrote it down wrong or some joker was enjoying watching me chase my tail.

I knew I had let my hopes get out of control. If I didn't land more work in the next two weeks, I'd be forced to close my team-building facilitation business and crawl back to a soul-deadening job served up with a bonehead boss on the side. The memory of the phone call from my last decent client still stung. Budget slashed. Contract cancelled.

Then yesterday, like a winning lottery ticket dropping from the sky, this guy Lucca called. He said his group needed my help, but refused to give any details until we met, like it was top secret.

I looked back at the forest crowding the winding dirt lane that passed for a road and twisted my necklace chain around my finger. What kind of consultation could someone way out here want? White supremacists dealing with dysfunctional team communications? Woolly mountain men asking for leadership training? Toothless hillbillies needing conflict resolution coaching? I doubted any of them paid very well.

"Ms. Robertson?" a voice called from the building.

My head jerked around. The necklace chain snapped with a ping. I stared at the broken links in my palm.

"Are you Marilee Robertson?" A man stood in the

doorway—his slicked jet hair, expensive tan, and the fashionable thread of a beard outlining his jaw seemed more Miami than backwoods.

I pitched the mutilated necklace at the passenger's seat. "You must be Lucca." At his nod, I clamped my portfolio under my arm. As I scrambled after him, I sniffed myself on the way and hoping I didn't stink of Eau de Desperation.

I noticed a scar meandering down the back of his neck. It looked red and recent.

Lucca ushered me into a sparse, toothpaste-green office. "Nice to put a face with a name." He gestured at a man skulking in the corner. "Fleet, my assistant."

"Associate," Fleet barked back.

Fleet's shaggy hair, mind-of-its-own beard, and layers of GoreTex and fleece frayed around the edges made him look like he should be hugging every tree along the lane here. His startling amber eyes jabbed at me. "Lady, if I were you, I'd get out of here and go back to your nice life. Forget about us."

Sour perspiration saturated my armpits under my blazer. I glanced back at the door, wondering if I still had my high school 400 meter dash record time in me if things turned ugly.

I reminded myself that every project seemed to have at least one difficult character, who sometimes turned out to be the one who signed the checks. "Uh, nice to meet you both," I offered.

Lucca rolled his eyes. He sat and tapped the page of a magazine sprawled across his battered desk. "I believe you wrote this."

Purple ink circled *The Masters of Teams: What We Can Learn from Wolves*. I'd written the article for a journal of minimal distribution and liberal publishing guidelines.

"You seem to know a lot about wolves," Lucca said.

I sat on a metal folding chair and straightened right up on the cold seat. The chair legs grated on the chipped linoleum. "A bit."

My stomach rumbled with a sinking feeling. My article research consisted of a bit of Googling, an afternoon in the library, and watching my dogs. A Rhodes Scholar of wolves I wasn't.

"I'd like you to help my group with some teambuilding, help us be like the wolves in your article."

I smiled. Finally, something that felt part of a normal business meeting. "Certainly." I opened my portfolio and assumed "the position"—pen at the ready, leaning forward, nodding sagely.

Lucca continued. "I'm the new leader of our group, less than a year. The transition hasn't gone as well as I'd like."

"The last guy died," Fleet added. "Suddenly."

He glowered at me. I stared back, wondering what power game was going on between these two. When Fleet's glare edged over the line from impassioned to Unabomber-disturbing, I looked away.

Hoping Lucca signed the checks, I addressed him. "Tell me about your group."

He glanced at his manicured nails and polished them on his pink dress shirt. "We're a club, a hunting club, you might say."

Fleet whirled out of his corner. He crouched over Lucca and pounded on the desk. "Quit this stalling crap. Just tell her straight up."

I jumped. My chair squealed. Lucca shot to his feet. The men scowled at each other, nose to nose, faces taut. I looked from one to the other. A flicker of recognition from my article stirred at the back of my memory.

I closed my portfolio and rose from my seat. Promise of work or no, I had no desire to stay for a macho pissing contest. I'd been caught in the spray too many times.

"Wait." Lucca stopped me with his hand. "We'll pay you double. No, triple."

My eyebrows rose. I thought of my empty calendar, my stack of bills, and my hungry dogs. Triple. It could be enough to stay solvent and properly launch my business. I salivated over the thought of having a website, a real business office, and possibly a part-time assistant.

I lowered into the glacial chair and pushed my hair behind my ears, once, twice, three times. A nervous gesture. "What should you tell me?"

Lucca's eyes widened as if he'd been goosed by an electric fence. "Your ears." He fixated on them in fascination.

I smoothed my hair back over the sides of my head and squirmed in my seat, self-conscious of my pointed ears. "Runs in my family. You should have seen my grandfather's."

Lucca wrinkled his nose and sniffed at me.

What the hell?

Fleet pounced forward and leaned close, pinning me in my chair. "*I'll* tell you what the deal is. We are"—he pulled his lips back and bared his teeth in what I took to be a grin—"werewolves. We change into wolves. Full moon, fangs, all that. Our club is for werewolves."

My pen slipped through my fingers and clanked on the floor. The warmth drained from my body. "W-w-werewolves?" Who says insane things like that? I didn't care if Fleet signed every check from now until my retirement, I couldn't work with someone who got their jollies from abusing consultants like this.

Lucca whispered through clenched teeth, "You're scaring her. Let me handle this."

Fleet stepped behind Lucca, lips pressed together in a white line, eyes blazing with defiance. I appealed to Lucca with a pleading look, hoping for the voice of reason, for him to finish the joke so we could get back to talking business.

Lucca rubbed the scar on the back of his neck. "It's true. We're werewolves. We hunt here. It's a stocked compound, secured for the safety of others so no one gets hurt. We're a registered pack with the American Werewolf Federation. It's all official. Public safety is our mission and main concern."

"Werewolves?" Were they both delusional? Was I? How did people who thought they were werewolves get organized across the nation into a federation? Facebook?

My mouth tasted of dirty, rust-colored, deep desert sand. I wanted to catapult out the door but my legs wouldn't move. "Werewolves? Real werewolves that attack and eat people?" I imagined Fleet flossing bloody meat out of his deranged smile. My stomach turned inside out.

"No, no." Lucca waved his arms. "We don't attack people. We hunt animals. In a secure environment. It's a stupid stereotype we constantly fight. We don't hunt people."

"Well, we try not to," Fleet added.

I leapt to my feet. My portfolio thunked on the floor. My papers swished into a version of fifty-two pick up.

Total kooks. Raging lunatics. Absolute bonkers. Nut jobs were impossible to work for and even harder to get them to pay you. My website, my assistant, my office, my thriving practice all flushed down the commode before my eyes.

I shook my head no and herded my papers into a pile. "Sorry. I can't help you. Gotta go." I needed to get back to my dogs to make sure they got fed, back to my life to make sure it got lived.

"Can't or won't?" Fleet asked. "Tell her what happened. She'll change her mind."

Lucca rubbed his scar again. "Yes, well, last month, we were out for our usual hunting party. And there was ... an incident."

I slung my purse over my shoulder. I didn't want to hear any more about werewolves or werewolf incidents. I bolted to the door like an espresso-fueled two-year-old. Lucca rushed to block me.

"I told you no one would touch this." Fleet crossed his arms. "Go on, lady, back to your presumably safe, civilian life. Don't worry about us. We'll figure it out eventually. There may be causalities, but hey, we'll figure it out."

Lucca pressed his palms together as if in prayer. "We wouldn't normally ask an outsider, but we really need help. You seemed to know about us, seemed able to help us. Please, it's a matter of grave public safety and the safety of our club members."

I narrowed my eyes and considered a knee to Lucca's groin. I hip-checked him instead. Thank you, college intramural broomball. He lunged sideways enough for me to wrench the doorknob open.

"We'll be in touch," Lucca called through the gaping door.

My high school coach would have been proud. Hurtling to the car, I think I beat my old record.

#

Two weeks later, I paced in front a hotel conference room window. I twisted my new necklace chain around my finger, thought better of it, and ran my hand through my hair instead. How could I have agreed to take on their bizarre werewolf teambuilding project? I fished my cell phone out of my purse and stared at it, considering if I should ring Lucca and call it off. I could tell him I had a debilitating migraine or a fatal case of fleas.

I hadn't meant to say yes. But the fourth time Lucca called, my mother had been reading from her latest help-wanted website. "Here's one, dear. Receptionist at the Pussycat Place. Good pay. Doesn't working in a shop with sweet little kitty cats sound nice?"

"It's a strip club, Mom."

It had been a weak moment. "Okay, I'll do it," just slipped out. And here I was at this hotel, ready for my first meeting.

"Anything else I can get you?" A chubby teenager with a catering name-tag had sneaked in behind me.

I took a quick check—a table, two chairs, drinks and snacks. I always started my projects by conducting one-on-one interviews with team members to discover potential issues and get to know the group. Usually I found this step exhilarating. Today I felt jumpy.

Lucca strutted through the door. "You're here. I worried you might not show."

I thrust the phone into my jacket and pumped Lucca's outstretched hand. "Everything looks good." I gestured at the room set-up.

Catering Boy nodded and trundled out behind his cart. Lucca ogled him, a ravenous gleam clouding his eyes. I shivered. Did he look at me that way when I left the room?

I giggled like a moron. "I have to admit, I'm a little nervous. Hoping you all won't bite. Glad there are snacks."

Lucca cleared his throat. "I wanted to apologize for our last meeting."

"Fleet already called and said he was sorry about how he acted."

"No, not Fleet. Me." Lucca rubbed his scar. "I was checking you out."

My mouth opened, but formed no sound. My cheeks blazed. I didn't need a romantic complication. Plus, he didn't remotely seem my type, and I had recently been through a feeding frenzy of a breakup. But he did fill out his navy blazer and light blue golf shirt in a way that could make me howl in the right mood. "I'm flattered."

"I'm sorry; I didn't mean it like that. Not that you're not attractive. But I already have a girlfriend."

"Oh." How embarrassing. And annoying. And vaguely disappointing. Where the heck did werewolves find girlfriends, anyway?

"It's your ears. Pointed ears are sometimes werewolf sign. The major test is here." He tapped his nose. "I can recognize other weres by smell. I have to admit, I sniffed you out."

So that's what he was doing. "Well, am I werewolf material?"

Lucca frowned at me. "You still don't believe we're really werewolves, do you?"

As hard as I tried to keep my face neutral, I'm sure it was clear I wasn't convinced. But I'd promised myself to keep an open mind and at least not say out loud how utterly the-moon-is-made-of-green-cheese preposterous it seemed. At least not until I got paid. "I believe that you believe."

"Just because we've done a good job keeping ourselves hidden doesn't mean we aren't real. I'm sure you believe in lots of things you can't see."

I smiled. The opening I needed. "Maybe it would help if I could see it. You mentioned problems with your hunts. In addition to interviews, I'd like to observe you and the group in action, on a hunt. See how you interact."

"Too dangerous." Lucca shook his head. "Hunts are unpredictable. If we get the scent of a human..." He shook his head more violently. "No. Our liability won't cover it if something goes wrong."

Liability for werewolves? Where do you get that?

Fleet entered behind Lucca, smiling his painful grin. "Maybe she could." His amber eyes glittered with an idea. "What if she covered herself with a wolf skin? It could mask her scent."

"Like a sheep in wolf's clothing?" I laughed at my own joke. "Actually, I was thinking of something easier. Video. Strap a camera onto one of you and I can watch the video later."

Lucca nodded. "That we can do." He nudged a piece of paper at me. "For today, here's the interview schedule."

I counted thirteen people on the list, including Fleet and Lucca. It just had to be thirteen. I scanned the names. At the last one, my breath caught in my throat and my heartbeat leaped like a dog after a Frisbee.

Doug McMillan.

It couldn't be him. Surely other Doug McMillans existed in the world. It couldn't be Doug "Flaming Jerk" McMillan, my boyfriend who recently became my ex. I prayed through gritted teeth for an elderly, balding Irish guy.

"This..." I pointed at his name. I couldn't say it.

"Doug? He's our Security Officer." Lucca drew his eyebrows together. "Do you know him?"

"Maybe."

"He's about my height, curly reddish hair, little goatee, works at a printing company, mountain bikes a lot? That Doug McMillan?" Fleet asked.

My Doug. I felt less rattled by the fact my ex could be a werewolf than the idea that I would have to face him and be "client nice."

A curly-haired young woman poked her head in the door, bringing me out of my shock. "Is this ... oh, Lucca. Hi, Fleet. Good, I'm in the right place." She smiled wide and bright as a sugar sand beach. "I'm Brenda. I think I'm first on your list." She inclined her head to just this side of winsome. I liked Brenda immediately.

#

The interviews flowed smoothly, except for the last one with Dork-Butt Doug, which ended up less an interview and more an hour-long tirade from me about how this werewolf stuff explained his frequent date no-shows, questionable hygiene, and why he was so meat-obsessed, but not any of the other hundreds of problems between us or why he refused to move in with me. Caca-For-Brains endured it with uncharacteristic meekness.

In the rest of the interviews, I tried not to ask questions about the how and why of werewolfry, except how it applied to their group interactions. But a couple of members projectile vomited their life stories all over me, as if relieved and happy to talk to anyone. I wanted to wash up afterwards.

Later that night, freshly showered and a chilled pinot grigio in hand, I summarized the interview results into bullet points.

- Club members came from every walk of life, economic status and age category. Demographically, there were six men, six women, plus Doug the Dillweed. None were related, although there was one married couple.
- The monthly hunt was the club's primary focus. Just before dusk of each full moon, they gathered. After shape shifting, which one person described as "like scraping all your skin off," their instincts took over. They had to hunt, kill and taste blood before they could shift back. If they didn't, they would eventually change back into human form, but it took longer and some wolf yearnings lingered. Human

blood was forbidden. Brenda explained, "As weres, we crave human flesh and blood like crack addicts. But if we ever taste it, then game over. Wolfsville forever. The human who is you is devoured by the animal. I think that would so suck. None of us wants that. We want more than anything to stay human."

• They all revered the previous leader, a loveable old fart who had been the founder of the club and an officer in the national werewolf association. Members all joined *this* club because he personally recruited them. He scoured the bowels of destitute missions and eyed the crowds of the Aspen elite to flush out and handpick potential members. He had died at an advanced age under mysterious circumstances.

• The other group members didn't trust Lucca. Few understood the former leader's choice of Lucca as his successor, since Lucca was a club newcomer. And the old man hadn't articulated the reasons for his choice before his death. A few thought Lucca was involved in the old man's death and that's how Lucca acquired his scar.

• No one wanted to talk about "the incident" at their last hunt. Fleet implied that a pesky group of local high school students had learned their lesson to stay away from the compound. Apparently, it was a close call but no one got seriously hurt. "Unfortunately," he added.

Reading over my findings, I admitted I was intrigued. I pretty much liked everyone, except for Dough-Head Doug. A group of stable, interesting, thoughtful, funny, caring people—the kind of group I'd like to be a member of myself. Although money was my first motivator, it seemed this would be a challenging, fun project, as well.

And I had already concocted ten ways to torture Candy Ass throughout the whole thing.

A shadow passed over my self-satisfaction. I realized Lucca hadn't answered my question about his sniff test. Did he think I was or wasn't a werewolf? And what if he thought I was?

#

A week later, I sat at the back of the American Werewolf Federation (AWF) Rocky Mountain Chapter meeting room, balancing my portfolio on my lap while taking notes. Club members circled a folding table, droning on about financial balances, national organization requirements, training events, blah, blah, blah, as Lucca crisply marched through their business agenda. I considered passing the time by doodling my dogs gnawing on Doug's ass.

I glanced at my watch. One hour down and thirty minutes to go until I fit the cameras to video the "hunt." I still didn't believe the whole changing-into-wolves-on-steroids story. I'd seen a reality show about vampire role-playing clubs where members sported stage names like Vladimir and Elvira and sipped drinks while telling stories about their supposed blood-sucking exploits. I expected my new friends would do the same while running around the woods under the full moon. Quirky, but not deadly.

Besides, if they were real, then that meant I might be...

A yapping cough interrupted Lucca's monologue and snapped my attention back to the meeting. Lucca's barking coughs echoed in the room's linoleum starkness. He convulsed in a hacking fit. He stopped, panting and wheezing, and tore at the collar of his silk t-shirt.

Dear God, was he hurt?

Lucca's body knotted with another attack. These coughs sounded deeper, more like a growl. The group gawked at Lucca, stiff in their chairs as corn-starched librarians. Why didn't they do something?

I stood. "He's choking!"

Lucca's rumbling coughs escalated to a continuous plaintive howl. It sucked the warmth out of my body down to my bones. Everyone jumped away from the table.

Lucca hunched over and gasped, his face contorted. He raised his arm and pointed a finger at me. "Get ... her ... out ... of ... here," he croaked.

"Security, Doug, take care of it," Fleet said. "Escort her outside the gate."

Why was everyone backing away? Lucca needed help. "I know the Heimlich." I took a step toward Lucca.

"Doug. Now!" Fleet yelled.

In the three steps it took Doug to cross the room, Lucca leaped onto the table, landing on all fours. He vaulted, bashing all the furniture over. He launched himself at me.

As Lucca hurled through the air, time distorted and elongated, allowing me to behold his transformation. Hair bristled from every pore, sprouting like a time-lapse, life-sized Chia pet. Lucca's shoulders distended and his limbs twisted. His pants split and fell away. Claws tore through his fingertips. The skin of his face roiled, expanding and contracting, an earthquake of changing topography. Ghost-white fangs cracked through his skull. It was horrible and wondrous at the same time. I couldn't breathe. I couldn't look away.

And then, time heaved forward as if catching up. It compressed into a smear of motion.

A body rammed into me. My head smacked against the floor. My vision clouded. A weight sat on my chest and pinned me down. I wriggled and flailed. I wasn't going to let that mouth-breathing hairball take a bite out of me.

"It's me," Doug whispered in my ear. "Let's get you out before he's done changing."

Cloth ripped. Doug winced. He rolled off of me and grabbed at his arm.

And then I saw what Lucca had become. He towered, half again as tall as a man. Paws the size of plates hung almost to his ankles. His arms and haunches creased with muscle. The snout, the fangs, the claws, the physique embodied the archetype of the feared and monstrous werewolf. His yowl mutated into a keen that froze my soul.

"Dear God, it's true." My voice trembled with realization. Humankind's blackest fears stepped out of the shadows and into my reality. It shook all I had ever believed true. What other supposedly fictitious creatures strolled around in the flesh down countless main streets amongst us clueless mortals?

Lucca's saliva dripped a stain onto my shirt.

Doug scrambled to his feet. He grabbed me around the waist and lugged me out the door. Lucca bayed after us.

Outside in the woods, I shoved Doug away. I bent over, hands on my knees until my huffing and puffing subsided. I straightened. The blood still pounded in my ears. A dizzying current of adrenaline soared through my veins. Was it the fear? The thrill?

Whatever. What a rush.

"Oh my God. Oh. My. God," I said to no one in particular. "It's for real. Straight out of the storybooks. A whole world nobody knows about except me. This is *so* cool." I felt giddy as a child standing before the gates of Disney World.

Doug tugged me toward the fence. "You, outside. Now."

As he dragged me by the arm, I gave him a raking gaze, head to toe, as if we'd just met. Everything about him seemed changed. Like the clearing of an Etch-a-Sketch, my animosities toward him vanished. "So, you do that too, change like that? You did it while we were, you know, together?"

He nodded and dropped my arm. "Couldn't tell you." He peered at the fading light dappling through the tree cover and scratched his shoulder. "I feel it coming on. Don't have much time. Gotta get you outta here."

"But my video, I need to take care of the cameras."

"I'll do it." He turned toward the gate.

I'd forgotten how cute he could be when he was worried—the pinch between his eyebrows, the pouty purse of his lips, even his chopped speech. A quiver raced through me at the thought of watching them while they hunted. It felt delicious being a voyeur of their hidden world.

I fell in step beside Doug. "Can I watch the hunt through the fence?"

"Too near. We could still smell you." He closed his eyes and inhaled. The edges of his lips curved in a slight smile. "Your smell is stronger even now." He picked up the pace. "As much for our good as yours. Too tempting."

"I'm too tempting, hmm?" I smiled warmly and threaded my arm through his. Feelings gushed through me. He was suddenly so ... hot.

Part of me twitched in horror that I crooned at a man whom I had offered yoga classes to so he'd learn how to stick his head up his own ass where it belonged. Part of me remembered a Psych 101 phenomenon about attractiveness increasing due to sharing stressful incidents. And part of me told the rest of me to quit being such an analytical know-it-all and jump him right there.

I noticed a rivulet of blood snaking around his forearm. "Lucca got you pretty good. Looked like he was ready to tear you apart."

Doug watched the ground as we walked. "Weres rarely attack other weres. He was after you."

I raised an eyebrow and looked sideways at him. "I guess that means you saved me."

Doug assumed his adorable "aw shucks" look. "Maybe." He stopped at the gate and hesitated. "You know, Mari, I wasn't the one who called it quits."

I turned on a syrupy smile and tilted my head. "I know. Maybe I was wrong." I stood on my tiptoes and landed a slow, juicy kiss on the surprised "oh" of his lips. I brushed my fingertips across his cheek for good measure. Resist that, Wolfie Boy.

A spasm rippled through him. "You gotta go now." He pushed me through the gate and locked it behind me. "Go straight to your car and peel outta here. Promise?"

I winked at him between the chain links. "Promise."

#

A tumultuous week later, I sat in the toothpaste-colored office reviewing the video of the club's hunt with Lucca.

"See this?" I pointed at my laptop screen. "The rest of the group looks at Fleet for the okay before they follow you? And here." I fast forwarded to another scene. "See the confusion? You go one way and Fleet goes another."

I recognized Doug on the screen by the way he hung his head and paced. He looked at Lucca, then at Fleet, then back again.

I bit the inside of my lip. I still mooned over Doug a few late and lonely nights when my dogs weren't looking.

On the video, a deer ran in front of Doug, saving him from having to choose between Lucca and Fleet. Doug loped after it. Everyone else chased after him.

I clicked pause before it got to the gutting and bloody gorge-a-polooza part. It had almost made me yak up a hairball at the first viewing.

I tested an observation with Lucca. "I noticed you never looked back to see if anyone followed you. At times you ended up alone."

He ran his fingers through his hair. "The alpha is supposed to lead and that's it, no questions. A pack can't survive if it doesn't follow its alpha."

He leaned back in his chair. "A friend warned me when I took over for my uncle, said she'd had the same trouble with her coven."

"Like in *witches'* coven?"

Lucca gave a slight smile. "There are lots of alternative lifestyles out there if you know where to look. Witches, fairies, goblins, those kinds of things. Worlds beyond what normal people see." He nodded as if a thought occurred to him. "I should tell her about all of this; she'd be interested how it turned out. At the time, I laughed at her."

Lucca's jaw clenched. He pressed his lips together and his hands gripped into fists. But the tension didn't reach his eyes. They reflected sadness and regret. He sighed and seemed to shrivel a little. "I didn't know it was so bad."

I sat in the icy folding chair. Inwardly I smiled while I waited for the inevitable next words. This was my favorite part. The turning point. Clients had to go through a process of discovery and recognition, fully feeling the pain of their situation, before they were ready to make changes. Usually they asked for teambuilding hoping I could "fix" everyone else. It always came as a shock when they figured out they were at the heart of the problem.

I could see these realizations etching the worry lines on Lucca's face. He opened his mouth. I slid forward in my seat.

Go on, say it. Just say it.

"What can I do? Can you help me?" he asked.

New taglines for my brochure formed in my imagination: *Marilee Robertson, consultant extraordinaire to the worlds beyond.* My dream blossomed exponentially before my eyes. Why, maybe I wouldn't even have to shave my legs so often ... and there was Doug.

I grinned in satisfaction and slid a paper with a bulleted list of recommendations across the desk. "Absolutely."

Barb A. Smith, like her story's protagonist, runs her own business providing team building, strategic planning and leadership training consulting, which she has been happily and profitably doing for over 20 years. In that time, she has never knowingly consulted with or met a werewolf, although she has had a few wild clients. In her writing career, Barb has written several short stories and is finishing her second fantasy novel, A Grain of Truth.

The Nu Tao Café
by Judy Metz

Theresa decided the only thing more humiliating than sleeping with her ex-husband was letting him con her into loaning him money. Again. Telling Amy wasn't such a hot idea, either.

"How could you be so stupid?" Amy repeated for the third time, coming out of the bathroom stall and glaring into the mirror as Theresa applied lipstick.

"Even when I thought I was going to die of loneliness, I never returned a single one of his calls, and it's been over three weeks since the divorce," Theresa said.

"Not that you're counting or anything."

"It's just that… I mean, when I came home and found him sitting there… well, it just happened, that's all."

"Do you want that scumbag back in you life?"

"No!" How had she ever deluded herself that telling Amy would help? Some best friend. Removing a brush from her purse, Theresa began to arrange her hair. No amount of make-up would hide the puffiness in her eyes from hours of crying. She pulled a rubber band out of her purse, looped it through the button hole of her skirt and wrapped it around the button, giving herself some extra inches at the waist. All her skirts and pants seemed too tight lately.

"Hey, I'm telling you for your own good." Amy paused, then said more gently, "I like your hair blonde better than that last auburn you tried. What's the new color called?"

"Paradise Platinum." Theresa blew her nose. Her current psychologist had advised Theresa to nurture herself by taking special care of her body.

So since the divorce, she had spent at least an hour a day curling and styling her hair and applying various masks, moisturizers and toners to her face. Her bathroom now held an impressive array of beauty products, but her hair made her feel silly, and her skin refused to glow. She felt no prettier or happier.

"We need to hustle. You'll feel better after some lunch," Amy said, patting Theresa's arm.

"Look, Amy, I think I need some time by myself."

"Don't be stupid. Or should I say more stupid? You need people around who care about you right now."

Theresa forced a smile. "We're going to be working in the same office all afternoon. You can comfort me some more then." She strode briskly away, escaping down the stairs rather than riding the elevator as usual. A walk in the spring air and lunch somewhere other than her regular Denny's might lift her mood. Maybe if she just started doing everything differently, she could get a grip on her life...

Amy was right. Why hadn't she demanded her ex's key? Again.

"Stop it," she mumbled, knowing that rehashing the details for the fortieth time that morning would not help. She turned one corner then another, moving into an unfamiliar part of Denver. Funny how she'd worked here for years and walked only certain streets.

Several minutes later, she paused under a crabapple tree covered with white blossoms and surveyed the street before her. Small shops and restaurants stood shoulder to shoulder. Many seemed to have apartments or offices upstairs. More blooming trees grew along the sidewalks. A slight breeze showered her with petals. She smiled, caught in the moment.

To her right hung a wooden sign with a dragon outlined in gold. Beneath the sign stood a red door with a menu tacked to it. She rarely ate anything but a hamburger and fries for lunch, but her new resolve to behave differently compelled her to turn the brass handle. A cluster of tiny bells suspended from the door by tasseled gold cords jingled.

The sound seemed to reverberate inside her as she descended a steep flight of stairs and emerged in a windowless room.

A round table set for ten dominated the center of the room, and empty booths covered in red vinyl lined the walls. Oriental music tinkled in the background, and the bubbler in an aquarium gurgled. She glanced around, surprised no hostess greeted her and hurried her to a table. Theresa was alone except for the black and orange koi circling in their tank. Maybe the place wasn't open. She didn't have much time for lunch. Should she leave?

The beaded curtain covering a door that must lead to the kitchen quivered, then slid apart to reveal a diminutive woman with wispy white hair. She approached with short, mincing steps that reminded Theresa of foot binding.

"I glad you choose Nu Tao Café," the woman said. She bowed, then inspected Theresa silently until Theresa felt her scalp prickle. She wondered if she was expected to bow back.

"I seat you in south, direction of heart," the ancient woman said, motioning to a booth and smiling so that the creases in her face seemed to lift and fold in on themselves like yellowed silk.

#

Theresa leaned back, her breathing slowing as she savored the spiciness of her Kung Pao shrimp. She surveyed the empty room. A restaurant with food this good wouldn't remain undiscovered long. In a city as large as Denver, privacy was a privilege to be cherished. She sighed. Privilege, smivilege. One thing she didn't need was more time alone. But it was a relief not to have Amy babbling and giving her advice.

"For you, two fortune cookie," the old woman whispered, holding out a silver tray with the bill and the cardboard-like confections Theresa hated.

Theresa shook her head, motioning to her thick middle. "I'm on a diet."

"You read and eat," the woman said more loudly and shoved the tray toward Theresa. A moment ago, the woman had seemed like a doddering grandmother. Now she bristled with the furious energy of an outraged oriental goddess.

Theresa forced herself to smile and broke open one cookie. She hated herself for being intimidated by such a tiny person. The hand-written fortune read: *Help your friend.*

Right, thought Theresa. Would loaning your ex your savings qualify? She had never gotten a hand-written message in a cookie nor one that seemed like a command before. Maybe the pushy little waitress wrote them. Keeping her eyes down, Theresa laid her credit card on the bill.

"Two." The woman scowled and motioned toward the second cookie.

Hating herself for being such a pushover, Theresa opened the other cookie. *Change your locks.*

"Now eat," the woman commanded.

Theresa swallowed her self-loathing and obeyed.

"You come next week." The woman jabbed her finger at Theresa.

These folks really needed to work on their customer relations.

#

Theresa gasped for breath as she climbed the fifth and last flight of stairs. Tomorrow she would complain about the broken elevator. She fumbled in her purse for her key. The purse started to slide out from under her arm. She grabbed for it, and the mail she held in her left hand fluttered to the floor. Her sack of groceries tipped to the side in slow motion, spilling the open bag of Chewy Cheese nuggets and popping open a container of eggs. One rolled across the hallway. Several smashed, the viscous liquid soaking the mail littering the carpet.

Hell, what more could go wrong?

Then the barking started. What was a dog doing in her apartment? It was growling now and seemed to be throwing itself against the other side of her door. It sounded big.

The door across the hall opened, and Mrs. Grabon peered through the crack bound by the security chain. "I've heard barking all day." Her narrow face and protruding eyes reminded Theresa of some ancient fairytale witch. "There are no pets allowed, as you well know." Theresa was sure Mrs. Grabon was menopausal and not taking her hormones regularly.

"There must be some mistake," Theresa said. She dropped to her knees to search for her key in the mess of mail, groceries, and the contents of her purse as the barking grew frenzied. The damned animal wasn't going to let her into her own apartment. Sweat stood out on her forehead, and her limp curls clung to her neck. Where was her key? The cheese snacks crunched underfoot. She fumbled in her purse again. With a mumbled oath, Theresa dumped the remaining contents of her purse on the floor and retrieved her key from among the fragments of the obscenely orange junk food.

"I'm afraid I'll have to report you to the building council."

"Why don't you just do that," Theresa said between clenched teeth.

The door banged against the inside wall as Theresa glared down at a wire-haired terrier. The small dog danced around the foyer, barking and growling. "And you, whoever you are, shut up!"

The dog retreated behind the couch while Theresa gathered the scattered groceries and kicked the door shut. As she dropped everything on the kitchen table, she saw the note and a bag of dog food.

Theresa,
Johnny's taking me to Vegas. Thanks for watching Aster.
XXOO,
Laurie
p.s. Aster loves to take walks.

"That's it! Too many people with too much access to my space," Theresa shouted, then grabbed the yellow pages from the cabinet and paged through to locksmiths.

The dog cocked its head and eyed her warily as she finished her call. "Now you," she said, frowning at him. "I suppose if I don't walk you, you'll pee on the rug. I bet you already have."

\#

The summer evening was warm, but a breeze ruffled the ornamental grasses by the entrance to the park. The dog was too busy chasing smells to bark any more, and Theresa felt the muscles in her neck relaxing as she followed the terrier toward the Platte River. She drifted along, allowing him to pull her every which way. Kids chased each other and lots of folks threw balls or Frisbees for their dogs or sat enjoying the deepening twilight. She realized that, although she had chosen her apartment for its proximity to the park a year ago, this was the first time she'd walked here.

Snarling and the jerking of the leash exploded her reverie. The damned dog was attacking something that looked like a powder puff. "Stop that, you idiot!" She dug in her heels and grabbed Aster's collar. As she hauled the dog back, an attractive blond-haired man scowled at her.

"He's not mine," Theresa said. "I mean, a friend left him with me, and I'm not sure…" With a disgusted look, Blond-and-Handsome scooped up the powder puff and strode off.

"Terriers can be a handful," a man in running shorts offered as he jogged in place. His dog looked identical to Aster. "If I don't run Caesar at least three miles every night, he redecorates the apartment while I'm at work."

"Run? You can't be serious," she said.

He laughed and came to a standstill. "They're great dogs, but hard to keep in an apartment. Michael Flanagan," he said, holding out his hand.

"Theresa Dubois." His grip was warm and made her hand feel small. To her disgust, she noticed that the dogs were sniffing each other's asses and wagging their tails.

"Looks like your dog has made a friend. Maybe Caesar and I will see you tomorrow."

She admired Michael's butt as he jogged off and enjoyed a little thrill of pleasure just before Aster wrapped the leash around her legs.

#

"Laurie, this is Theresa," she said, watching Aster chew one of her new Italian boots. She hated talking to answering machines, she hated the damned dog that was destroying her possessions one by expensive one, and she hated her life. "It's been over a week, and you need to pick up this animal, or I'll take him to Dumb Friends." She snapped her cell phone closed. "Or possibly kill him."

The terrier dropped the mangled piece of leather and disappeared into the bedroom. He returned with the leash in his mouth and his whole back end wiggling. "All right! All right! Let me at least change out of my work clothes."

In the park she practiced running twenty steps and walking forty as her exercise book suggested. In spite of constant vigilance on her outings with Aster, she hadn't seen Michael since the first night. Just as well, since the unaccustomed exercise made her sweat like a sumo wrestler. She had given up doing anything with her hair except pulling it up off her neck. Her roots were showing; clearly it was time to dye her hair, but she figured if she didn't look in a mirror, she wouldn't see her roots showing.

As they turned away from the river and headed home, Aster tugged so hard that, before she could get control, he dragged her past the fountain and up two flights of stairs to the platform that overlooked Union Station.

How could a little dog be so strong? He started down the other side. After they dodged around a man carrying a briefcase, Theresa grabbed an ornamental lamp post. "Stop! I mean it." Aster continued to pull until he slipped his head out of the collar. "Come back here!"

An older couple turned to stare. "My dog..." She smiled sheepishly, holding up the leash. She jogged after Aster, who sat waiting for her at the corner.

That's it, she vowed to herself, he goes to Dumb Friends tomorrow. *Oh, God, what if he gets hit by a car!* She ran after him, ignoring the stitch in her side. When she neared the corner, Aster trotted off. She spotted him sitting under the gold dragon sign. But when she reached out to grab him, a tall woman exited the red door, and Aster ducked in. She swore under her breath. At least now she had him cornered.

The glow of what must have been fifty Chinese lanterns illuminated the empty tables. Aster sat at the feet of the white-haired waitress. To Theresa's surprise, Aster sat up, then lay down and rolled over.

The ancient Chinese woman bowed to the dog. "Good boy. I bring treat."

"You," she added to Theresa and pointed to a booth on the south wall, "sit."

At least the waitress hadn't ordered Theresa to roll over and play dead.

As she sank onto the seat, Aster thrust his head against her leg. She could swear he was smiling. She rubbed his ears, too pooped to scold him.

The old woman returned with a dog biscuit for Aster and a bowl of hot-and-sour soup for Theresa. The steam rising from the rich, dark soup smelled divine.

"But I'm too…"

"Eat," the woman ordered.

Theresa was sure there was some health regulation against dogs in restaurants, but after all that running, it felt good to sit.

The woman disappeared and returned carrying the silver tray and two fortune cookies.

"I don't have any money," Theresa said, feeling the prickle of a blush in her cheeks. "I didn't intend…"

"Pay next time. Eat cookies now."

Theresa didn't argue. The first slip of paper read: *Buy shoes.* The second said: *Enroll in training.*

"As if I have the money or time," Theresa mumbled.

#

The Saturday morning sun warmed Theresa's shoulders as she jogged her third lap around the park. Aster trotted at her side, in a precise "heel" position. Her damp tank top clung to her back, but as she slowed to a walk, Theresa felt a deep contentment.

"Sit," she commanded and Aster dropped to his haunches. She smiled. That obedience class had really worked. Aster was good company, and he never gave her advice or told her she was stupid like some human friends. Over the last several weeks Theresa had dropped a full dress size and had given up calling Laurie. This was the improved version of her life, even if her florescent orange running shoes didn't match a single thing in her wardrobe.

"Hey, Ter, honey, what ya doin?"

Only one person called her Ter. Should she pretend she hadn't heard?

"Hey, babe, wait."

She turned and glowered at Harry, her ex-husband. Aster assumed a protective stance between her and Harry, then began to growl.

"I seem to be locked out of the apartment," he said. He gave her his goofy smile and shrugged.

"That's because I changed the locks."

"Hey, your hair's different." He reached out to fondle the pony tail that had poked out the back of her baseball cap.

She jerked away, and Aster howled, lunging for Harry's ankle.

Harry jumped back, kicking at the dog and missing. "Hey, what's with the dog?"

"He doesn't like you, and I don't either."

Aster's teeth tightened on Harry's pant leg. "Sit, Aster." The dog released Harry and obeyed but continued to growl.

"What the f—"

"Go away, Harry, and stay away. I want you out of my life."

"Is there a problem?" a deep male voice asked.

Theresa felt the tension drain from her jaw as she recognized Michael and his dog, Caesar.

"My former husband was just leaving."

Caesar positioned himself next to Aster and inspected Harry with his teeth bared.

"If you're finished here, Theresa, why don't you and Aster run the river path with me and Caesar?"

"I am definitely done here," she said.

"Maybe we can have lunch later," Michael said as they jogged away. "I found this great Chinese place."

After years as a cognitive coach and staff developer, Judy Metz learned that sometimes organizational or personal change requires a miracle. She continues to explore the magic of a characters' willingness to grow in her third novel, Enchantment for Breakfast. *It's also a central concept in The Nu Tao Café, her first published short story.*

Porter
by Alexei Kalinchuk

Porter did his drinking in a neighborhood spot called The Fancy Tiger until they shut it down a few years back. An absurd name, or perhaps not if you didn't think names meant anything.

Still, he missed it.

Lot of memories he made in that place.

So when they reopened it six months ago, he was looking forward to swimming up against the echoes of all those good times and the jukebox playing the old songs.

Except it wasn't like that now.

The night of the opening, a bunch of young people mobbed the place. They drank cocktail specials the color of industrial solvents, put them atop tiger-striped coasters. A live band banged out something that might've been music, while the bartenders, ladies all of them, wore orange cat ears.

"What've they done to it?" he asked himself, looking at all the movie posters they'd hung on the walls.

They should've left the damn bar closed.

\#

Finding a flyer for The Fancy Tiger on his front door a week after his visit, Porter crumpled it and cursed.

There were bars, then there were bars, and he remembered all the ones he'd been to, all their garish names. The Happy Fish. The Black Labrador. The Blue Ox Bar. And then the places with plain names. Morrison Tavern. River Inn.

Whoever bought The Fancy Tiger must've bought it for this reason alone. A name! Because it had a neon sign of a cartoon tiger wearing a top hat instead of a sign that said BAR.

What a reason to do anything.

#

He went back to The Fancy Tiger on another night. He had to; he had just so many memories of the place. Walking in, first thing he noticed all the dressy folks drinking white wine, talking on their cell phones right next to the smart-alecky kids with tattoos who wore the bar's t-shirt.

Bars shouldn't have t-shirts, they just shouldn't.

But at least they'd kept the painting.

It hung behind the bar over a shelf of bottles. It was a tiger coiled up on a ridge ready to leap on something. All the years of cigarette smoke had darkened the picture so that only the muzzle and part of the shoulder were visible.

Porter stared a long time at the tiger's fangs, admiring them.

#

Some people who now frequented The Fancy Tiger were the unfriendly ones who had become his neighbors. After most of his old neighbors had died or gone to nursing facilities, newcomers bought up their houses. Though he tried being personable, they didn't even return his greeting when he walked by while they washed their expensive foreign cars in their driveways.

They should be friendly to him, he decided. He didn't move to *their* neighborhood. They moved to *his* and caused *his* property taxes to rise.

One of the newcomers knocked on his door one day to tell him she was organizing a homeowners association and would he like to add his name to some list on her clipboard.

"I think I like how things are, actually," he told her.

"That's… I see…" She wrinkled her nose and left.

The newcomers looked like lawyers and professors and doctors.

The thirty-forty something ones did. The younger ones wore t-shirts with cartoon characters or swearing on them. They adopted slouching poses, pouted like they couldn't care less.

But they did.

One time Porter called the cops about the loud party in the house next door, and that homeowner, a kid, he came right over the next morning to talk. "You didn't have to do that. You could've told us we were too loud." The kid wore blue-tinted sunglasses like they did in the 70s, a too-tight shirt with Japanese writing on it and baggy pants that hung low enough to show the top of his underwear. "Anyway, aren't you retired? It's not like you have to go anywhere the next day."

"I still need to sleep," Porter said, and it was true.

He supposed the kid's clothes had something to do with fashion; a thing he'd never understood, though he once owned a fine hat everyone complimented him on. No one wore fedoras now.

The kid told him the police issued two citations, one for the noise, another because one of his friends' girlfriends was underage and drinking. The kid seemed mad about it. Porter couldn't see why. "If she's that young, then maybe she doesn't need to be drinking."

The kid sneered, said, "Fine. We can be like that. We can be just like that." Then he packed off to his house.

For weeks after that, Porter found empty beer cans and cleaned rib bones thrown into his backyard.

#

They'd invaded his neighborhood and his bar; sometimes they even swiped the parking space in front of his house. Porter wished for a means of revenge but all the time knew its futility. Change bullied anyone who resisted it.

But something spurred him to act one morning.

The kid next door's dog had gotten loose, turned up on Porter's porch just as he went to get his morning paper. Could you beat that? He took paper and dog into his house, meaning to show that damned kid he had no sense leaving his animal out.

But a few hours after he'd gotten the dog inside, he decided he wasn't giving it back. He liked its large brown presence. And it didn't bark. Must've been an injury or some throat cancer like what'd killed Porter's wife ten years back.

When the knock at the door came midday, Porter hid the dog in the back bedroom of his house before answering it.

"I'm looking for my dog. Have you seen him?" Today the kid next door wore a trucker's mesh-backed baseball cap that said CAT. How odd. Porter thought the kid worked in computers.

"What's he look like?"

"He's the only dog I have."

"It doesn't mean I know what he looks like," Porter said.

"Okay, he's brown. He doesn't bark."

"Why not? Factory forgot put in a 'woof'?"

"Just tell me if you see him." His disgusted neighbor left the porch then.

#

Porter started walking the dog in the early morning when his next-door neighbor would be asleep. The dog didn't pull at the leash or bolt towards his old home. Porter liked that. Still, all these lawyers and accountants taking their five a.m. jog worried him. He didn't want to be found out.

Didn't want to be labeled a dog thief.

#

A week after the dog had been with Porter, the next-door neighbor started posting *lost dog* flyers on nearby streets.

Porter harrumphed at that.

If the guy had really wanted the dog back, he wouldn't have waited a whole week before taking action.

Yet the flyers worried him.

He thought of the other day at the grocery store, how the HOA woman saw him paying for a twenty-pound bag of dog food. Though he'd smiled at her, waved, she frowned back. Probably because her idea failed.

Porter didn't want someone like her reporting to his next-door neighbor that he'd taken the dog.

So one morning he woke up even earlier than normal, so early that darkness hid the streets, and he ripped down several flyers. It only took a week to rip down every one in a five-block radius. Like the kid said, Porter was, after all, retired. He had the time to tear things down.

He only hated that it kept him from enjoying his new dog.

Porter liked to walk the dog up and down the hills of the nearby streets, like they were two adventurer-friends searching for a treasure they'd split.

#

And then came the day. While Porter practiced putting a golf ball into a glass on its side, someone knocked on his door. It could've been a Mormon or a salesman, but it wasn't.

The neighbor kid, his hair looking like he'd rubbed a raw egg in it from whatever pomade he used, glared at Porter, then pushed him aside and stomped past headed for the back bedroom.

"Hey! What do you think you're doing?" Porter said, but he already knew what had tipped the kid off. Yesterday Porter had noticed how sad the dog looked, so he opened the drapes for him.

Someone must've seen the dog in the window.

The neighbor kid returned from Porter's back bedroom holding the dog by the collar, mouthing off and calling him a thief. Rocket—what Porter ended up naming the dog—went along meekly. "You've got a lot of nerve stealing a dog. I should call the cops on you, old man."

Porter, the putter still in his hand from when he'd answered the door, listened to all the ugly slander the kid heaped on him. And he could've stood that.

But Rocket made these eyes at Porter and, though he'd never been the kind of man who thought he could tell what a dog was thinking, today he would've said yes, he knew the dog meant: *I don't want to go.* That clinched it; Porter swung his golf club.

His swing sliced the air. Pounded the kid in the shoulder and he fell over the dog cursing. Rocket yelped. The first sound Porter had ever heard him make. The second swing chopped at the kid's ankle, and he screamed. Porter fell back, frightened by that sound and his actions.

Holding his shoulder, the kid scraped himself off the floor, limped out of the house, waiting until he cleared the door before calling Porter a son-of-a-bitch and a whole lot worse.

After shutting the door, Porter turned to look for Rocket but didn't see him. Once he located the dog in the back bedroom, the animal shuddered at his touch. The poor thing was scared of him now. Oh, hell.

Later he heard some commotion out front, so he crept to the front of the house to peek out a window without parting the curtain. There they were. The neighbor kid and two of his scruffy t-shirt friends standing beside the HOA woman. So they all knew each other. Did that mean she told them about seeing him buy the dog food?

A police car pulled up after a few minutes.

Porter moved away from the front window and went to sit in a padded armchair, rubbed at his eyes. So tired today.

The police knocked and knocked on his door, but he didn't get up to answer. And explain what he'd done? He sensed a presence in the room. He turned and saw Rocket. From across the room they stared at each other while the policeman's knuckles played their stern music on the doorframe.

Alexei Kalinchuk, an active member in RMFW, was born in Mexico City and has lived in Los Angeles and Houston. He lives in Denver and has published several stories in literary magazines. He is currently working on a novel.

The Cowgirl and the Plum Crazy Purple B
by Jameson Cole

It was at a barroom dance hall when I first noticed Penny—standing beside me shuffling her feet to the music. Just a pip-squeak of a cowgirl—a young brown-haired lass who looked like she'd get asked for her ID if she ordered a Coke, though she'd have to be twenty-one to get into Lucky's. Her face was fresh and clean, somehow producing a tiny bunny nose with a half-dozen freckles on each cheek. A mischievous look curled up the corners of her mouth. Long hair danced around her shoulders, and she wore a Texas Rangers baseball cap, plain white blouse, and fraying jeans shorts whacked off above mid-thigh. A nice pair of slender legs tapered down into tan, well-worn working boots that might never have smelled polish.

At first I didn't want to have anything to do with her, figuring she was too young for me. But quicker than a cricket's chirp, she had me laughing, and before long we were slow dancing. One thing led to another and I soon had my hand on her butt hoping for further progress.

Of course, that's when I got into trouble, discovering the hard way she was my partner Frog's daughter, home from college, and that she'd be rodeoing with us this season. I disliked the idea entirely, figuring it would interfere with my hooking up with buckle bunnies, but I didn't have a whole lot to say about it.

Penny was a feisty critter, and as the rodeo season progressed, we had our share of arguments, even though I was a lot older—thirty to be exact—and I tried to treat her like my little sister and protect her from rodeo vultures like Arnold The Terminator Thompson. This wasn't an easy task, not by a long shot.

Anyway, we were all up in Greeley, Colorado working the Independence Stampede. Frog and I were rodeo bullfighters. Our job was to distract bad tempered bulls away from downed cowboys—to save their asses from dangerous hooves and savage horns. And Penny was competing in the barrel races.

Thirty minutes before the rodeo was to start, Penny and I arrived at Island Grove Park where the rodeo was held. The grounds were extensive and spacious, with a large outdoor horseshoe-shaped arena capable of seating ten thousand people. Even though it was early evening and still light outside, the stadium lights were on full bore and people were streaming in from everywhere.

"Frank!"

Turning, we saw Big Bob hurrying toward us, obviously upset about something.

Penny and I glanced at each other, wondering what was up.

The big man stood six-feet-four, his lanky bow-legs supporting two hundred-fifty pounds of satisfied belly. Almost hidden underneath was a huge, twenty-year-old belt buckle that proclaimed him a former World Champion steer wrestler. He wore a pearl-buttoned, long-sleeved white shirt, tight Wrangler jeans at least one size too small for him, and a tan Resistol hat over his balding head. An oval, fifty-ish face offered a naturally friendly smile.

I liked Big Bob. 'Course, everybody did.

Big Bob was the stock contractor for the Greeley Independence Stampede and our boss. He halted before us, huffing and puffing, his big chest heaving from the exertion, his squinty eyes flashing. "Where the hell is Frog?"

I shrugged. "He's here somewhere. He came on ahead."

Big Bob shook his head vehemently. "He ain't here. I've been looking all over for both of you. Damn!"

Both of us? "What's the problem?"

He looked me square in the eyes. "Can you drive four-up?"

Four horses hitched to a chuckwagon? "Sure. Why?"

The burly stock contractor turned in a circle, his eyes scanning obviously for Frog, then faced me. "The chuckwagon crews went out to dinner together and got some bad food. Damn near all of 'em are spewing their guts out right now."

"It isn't serious, is it?"

"They'll all live. But they ain't feeling much like tearing around the arena on a bouncing buckboard. I need two drivers or we'll have to cancel that part of the show."

Big Bob needed help. I nodded. "I'll drive."

"Won't do us no good to have one driver. Where in Sam Hill is Frog?"

Most likely he'd found himself a woman. But it was never a good idea to speculate to your employer about a missing pal. "He's probably here somewhere. He'll show up any minute."

Big Bob spun around in another circle, looking in vain for Frog. He threw his hands upward in frustration. "I can't count on that. I'm going to have to cancel the race and they'll be a passel of disgruntled folks—"

Penny stepped between us and looked up. "I can drive."

I'd almost forgotten she was here.

Surprised, Big Bob looked down at her skeptically. "You've driven a chuckwagon in a race before?"

Standing beside Big Bob, Penny looked no bigger than a freckle-faced tadpole wearing a Texas Rangers cap. "I can drive anything that rolls and runs."

She'd driven Big Bob's old tractor at his ranch plenty of times, spinning those huge back tires like a hot rod. "A chuckwagon race isn't the same as harrowing dirt in a corral. This is dangerous stuff."

Penny shot a dirty look at me. Her jaw tightened and she nodded with finality. "I'm racing. Right, Big Bob?"

Big Bob glanced at both of us in turn, then his eyes flashed decisively. "You're both racing. But I don't want either of you doing anything foolish and getting hurt. You hear?"

We both nodded.

He waved a hand in the general direction of the arena. "Hurry on over to the staging area and slip on their team colors, get familiar with the horses, and get ready to go."

Big Bob hurried off, his belly swinging from side to side with each step.

"I can drive anything that rolls or runs," I said, mocking Penny. "When did you ever race chuckwagons?"

Penny glared at me. "I raced powder puff two summers ago. It's no big deal."

"Powder puff! Ha! Girls racing girls. I told you this was dangerous and here you go getting yourself involved. You're the stubbornest pip-squeak I've ever known."

Penny brushed past me. "Don't call me pip-squeak. And twenty bucks says I beat your butt."

I called after her. "I don't want to bet."

Penny stopped and turned back to me, grinning. "Chicken!"

Thirty minutes later, Mexican trumpet music blared from the loudspeakers, and the Grand Entry got underway, with riders parading and cavorting spectacular saddled horses around the arena. The chuckwagon race would be the first competitive event, and the typically wild race with spills and mix-ups usually jump-started the crowd's blood coursing through their veins. Normally, there'd be eight wagons running four to a heat, with the two heat winners competing for the championship. But today, there'd only be one race—Penny's team against mine.

The two wagons Penny and I were going to drive stood side by side, mine with a red canvas cover, and Penny's with a purple canvas cover. Each wagon was a plain wooden box about three feet wide, a dozen feet long, with four spoked, iron-rimmed wheels.

And no brakes.

Already harnessed to each wagon was a team of four antsy thoroughbreds, stamping their feet, shaking their bridled heads and collared necks. Thoroughbreds know one thing and that is racing— every ounce of their body language said they were raring to go. To keep them steady, one of Big Bob's rodeo hands sat in each wagon, holding the reins.

I'd slipped on an inexpensive red hat, a red shirt, and a white neckerchief that matched the colors of my wagon, its name—Reeling & Rocking—emblazoned across the red canvas in white letters.

Along with her team members, Penny wore a purple shirt and white neckerchief. The name of her wagon—Plum Crazy Purple B— was scrawled across the purple canvas in giant white shaky letters, as if they'd been painted on the move. Her team members had given her a purple hat two sizes too big, and Penny had stuffed tissue inside the band to make it fit. She looked kinda cute in the purple shirt and tight Wrangler blue jeans.

Out of all those cowboys who'd been at the tainted dinner, Big Bob could scramble together only seven healthy outriders. Being one short, he'd enlisted his livestock manager Joe Simpson to fill out my team. I'd sat down at the back of my wagon with my four red-shirted outriders and gone over the details of the race.

We were just breaking up when I noticed a familiar figure approaching Penny. Arnold Thompson—a top fifteen National Finals Rodeo bull rider. Inexplicably, he was dating Penny. I had no use for Arnold. He liked to call himself The Terminator and he was hard on animals. Besides that, we'd had a couple of run-ins and he'd cold-cocked me a couple times—when I wasn't looking, of course.

Lanky, dark-haired, wearing black clothes and a black hat, his face was as rough-hewn as broken granite. That black-hatted scum obviously liked wearing black—even his Wrangler jeans were black. The color matched his soul.

Penny was at the front of her rig smooth-talking her horses, letting them get to know her. Arnold stopped behind her and put his hand on her shoulder, grinning as if there was some imaginary charm inside him. Penny turned and spoke to him.

Standing maybe twenty-five feet away from the two of them, I couldn't hear what they were saying, so I decided I might as well check on my horses, too. I walked forward, patting the nearest wheel horse, checking the leather harness rigging, keeping my hat down over my face, moving up beside the lead horses, edging closer, watching Arnold out of the corner of my eye.

The two of them seemed to be talking at the same time, and Arnold's grin was fading fast. His lips started to curl and a mean look appeared on his face.

Arnold's true self was emerging, his face filling with rage. Penny might be in trouble.

Cautiously, I edged closer, ready to step in if—

Arnold exploded. Reaching out, he grabbed her shoulders, shaking her violently, shouting, "Well, screw you, you little bitch!"

Turning, I yelled, "Arnold!"

His attention swung to me. He recognized me instantly.

Penny's knee elevated into Arnold's groin.

"Yeowww!" Arnold caved over, his hands going to his privates. He sank to his knees, moaning.

I strode firmly up beside Penny and stopped. Lord-a-mercy, this was a special day. Arnold had gotten his balls busted. And by Penny, no less. I wanted to put my thumbs in my belt, swell my chest, rock back on my heels, and grin. But it was too dangerous to gloat with Arnold around, even if ... oh, hell, I grinned anyway.

He looked up, still holding himself, his eyes filled with pain and hate. Filthy words spewed through his clenched teeth. "Damn you, bitch. Someday I'm going to spread your legs wide and screw your brains out."

Underneath her red hat, Penny's eyes flashed with anger. She balled her small hand into a fist, drew her arm back, and punched him in the face!

Preoccupied with his privates, Arnold hadn't seen it coming. He keeled over backwards, his hands going to his nose, moaning.

Penny stepped forward, fists clenched, ready to bust him again.

No one deserved it more than that foul mouthed SOB, but I put my hand out, staying her arm. "Hold on there, Penny. We don't want to hit the bastard while he's on the ground."

Penny shook my hand loose, but didn't try a second swing. "The hell I don't."

Around us, the outriders from both teams had gathered, a tougher bunch of boys than you'd ever want to meet. Joe Simpson scowled angrily. He liked Penny. And I'm sure he didn't like what Arnold had just said. Neither did I.

Arnold rolled to his knees, struggling to get up, one hand pinching his nose. Bright red blood ran over his fingers and dripped down onto his black shirt front. "You broke my nose!"

I reached down and grabbed Arnold by his collar and the back of his belt, hauling him to his feet and shoving him away from the wagons into a couple of the boys, one of them Joe Simpson. "You better git while the gitting's good."

Still holding his bloody nose, Arnold turned and yelled, his voice muffled and nasal. "I ain't never gonna forget this. I'll get even if it's the last thing I ever do."

Joe gripped Arnold's shoulder, hard, looking him straight in the eyes. "If you ever touch Penny again, *it will be the last thing you ever do.*"

Peering over his blood-streaked fingers, Arnold blinked, then his eyes turned white at the corners. He didn't say anything back to Joe.

Joe spun Arnold around and shoved him toward the arena, booting him in the ass.

All the outriders laughed as Arnold staggered to keep his balance.

Arnold glanced back, glaring with hatred, but didn't stop, limping along gingerly.

Beside me, Penny grabbed my arm, turning me to face her. "Don't ever step into my fight again. If I want someone hit, I'll be the one who hits 'em."

Trumpet music sounded again from the loudspeakers, signaling the finale to the Grand Entry. The outriders moved away from us, toward their horses. Already, participants from the Grand Entry were trotting their horses from the flood-lit arena. In a few seconds, we'd be driving our wagons inside.

I looked down at Penny's stubborn, angry face. She seemed a lot tougher now. Growing up, maybe.

The outriders had mounted up, their horses prancing. "We got to go," Joe called.

Penny and I walked past the horses, back toward the front of the wagons. "What was all that with Arnold?"

Penny stepped up on the front wagon wheel hub and climbed onto the wooden seat, taking the reins from the hand who then jumped down from the wagon. "I found out I couldn't trust him."

I climbed into the Reeling & Rocking wagon. Taking the reins, I called to her, "I told you that a long time ago."

Sitting down, Penny took the reins, expertly threading them under her hands, up through the fingers, then back down through the fists. She slapped the reins against the horses' backs. The thoroughbreds jumped forward, the wagon wheels rolling across the dirt, the noisy buckboard clattering and rumbling along, headed for the arena entrance.

I flipped my reins hard. My chuckwagon lunged forward, the horses eager to go. "Penny? What did Arnold do?"

She leaned to the side, looking around the purple canvas cover back at me, and yelled, "He's been bedding every bitch this side of Albuquerque."

We rolled into the huge U-shaped arena, Penny in the lead, snaking her team back and forth to get the feel of the chuckwagon and the horses used to her lead. Doing the same, I trailed behind her, eating the cloud of dust kicking up. I'd never seen Penny drive four-up before, but I had no doubt she knew what she was doing sitting up there in that seat.

Ahead, Penny's four purple-shirted outriders trotted their horses along side her chuckwagon, yelling, pumping up each other, getting the horses even more excited. Beside me, my outriders were doing the same. I felt a tingling in my body, needing the race to get started.

Overhead, blaring from the loudspeakers, the announcer's voice explained the race to the fans. What with all the noise of the chuckwagon, the horses' hooves pounding, and the outriders yelling, I could barely hear him.

We paraded past the grandstands, where our already assigned figure eight patterns had been set up, along with our simulated campstoves—small black twenty-gallon barrels with a four inch chimney welded to the top, from which poured dense black smoke from a lighted smoke bomb.

After we paraded in front of the stands, we turned our teams back to the grandstands near the bottom of the arena "U."

The race would consist of each chuckwagon team first running a figure eight pattern around two barrels out into the infield, then coming back to the track beside the stands and racing counter-clockwise around the entire half-mile track with the finish line in front of the grandstand.

Each pattern had two barrels we had to circle—the near one positioned thirty feet in front of the bucking chutes and the far barrel another seventy-five or so feet out into the infield. Penny would run the number one pattern on the right nearest the track. The number two pattern was thirty feet to the left of Penny's pattern, which meant I'd have extra track distance to run, but my figure eight pattern was shorter than Penny's to make it fair.

Penny and I turned our wagons away from the grandstand, pulling them along the right side of each barrel, stopping with each wagon's back wheels in line with the near barrels. All the outriders dismounted, leaving one to hold their mounts, and scurried into action.

In front of me, Joe Simpson grabbed the lead horses' bridles and squatted, using his weight to steady them. To the rear, an outrider pulled two six-foot tent poles from the wagon bed already attached to the canvas top-flap, quickly setting up a tent extending from the chuckwagon rear. The last outrider was assigned to "throw stove." He picked up the small black barrel with its smoking chimney and moved it over beside the tent. To my right, Penny's team had finished setting up their "camp" also.

"Hold your positions!" the announcer called.

We were seconds away from racing. My heart beat faster. I glanced quickly at Penny.

She winked at me and grinned broadly. Then she leaned forward, her body tensing, her hands holding the reins ready.

Overhead, the announcer's mellow twang rolled from the loudspeaker horns as he jawed on about the history of chuckwagons. "...when the West was young, and great cattle drives crossed the country, the chuckwagon crew prepared hearty breakfasts, then broke camp to hurry to the next camp to prepare the evening meals. Sometimes it was important to beat another outfit to the best camping spot."

"Bammm!" Up in the booth, the announcer fired a starter's gun.

Startled, my lead horses jolted a step, tossing their heads, lifting Joe clean off the ground as he clung to their bridles.

As the horses steadied, I glanced backward through the red canvas arch.

The "stove throwing" outrider at the rear of the wagon hoisted the smoking barrel onto his shoulder and tossed it through the canvas opening into the back of the wagon, the bed banging as it hit. The other outrider jerked down the two tent poles and threw them into the back, still attached to the top flap. "Go!" they chorused.

Simultaneously, up front, Joe released the lead horses' bridles, dodging out of the way, and I slapped the reins against the horses' backs, yelling at the top of my lungs in a raspy, coarse voice, "Gi-aattt!"

The horses broke fast, charging past Joe. In seconds, he'd be swinging up into his saddle to follow along, as all the outriders were required to be within a hundred and fifty feet of the wagons when the race was over.

Accelerating rapidly now, I focused on the far barrel set up in the infield, angling left of it, slapping the reins. Penny's team wasn't even in my peripheral vision. Hot Damn! The Reeling & Rocking wagon was in the lead and I meant to stay there.

I had twenty dollars riding on it.

I swung the horses wide left, then turned hard right to circle the far barrel. The turn as tight as I could make it, the rear wheels slid, spewing a shower of dirt.

We came out of the clockwise turn too fast, the rear wagon wheels slipping way out to the left. Penny's Plum Crazy Purple B wagon hove into view, rolling hard, heading straight for us. Her face bubbled with determination to catch up and she shouted to her horses.

Oh, Lordy! Our wagons were going to collide!

Turning my team further right, I slapped the reins across the horses' backs, needing them to accelerate to pull our wagon from danger.

Beneath me, the wagon rose, tilting up on its two left wheels. Desperately, I threw my weight to the right as a counter balance. We needed more speed or we'd flip over, right into Penny's team of horses. We needed more speed now! "Git! Haw!"

The horses strained, charging forward, pulling my wagon through the turn, balanced precariously on two wheels.

Ahead, Penny was turning her team to her right to swing around her barrel. The back end of her wagon began sliding, skidding across the loose soil headed straight for the side of my wagon. We were seconds from colliding.

"Go!" I lashed the reins again, feeling the horses surge ahead, straightening out of the turn.

My wagon slammed down on all four wheels, darting forward. Penny's wagon slid toward us, the back wheel showering us with a wave of dirt, missing us by inches. Purple-shirted outriders dashed along behind Penny's wagon. Mine were somewhere behind me.

We thundered toward the right side of the near barrel and I hauled the team hard left onto the half-mile track that circled the horseshoe arena. "Git, git, git!" I yelled, whipping the reins.

No longer having to turn, the thoroughbreds quickly gained their full stride, running full out, tails and manes streaming, racing along side the arena fence. The grandstands with their tall sky boxes flew past.

I guided the horses in a gentle arc toward the far right uppermost end of the arena "U," feeling good to be in the clear. Elated, I risked a glance backward.

My four outriders were keeping pace, fifty or so feet behind the wagon, galloping through the dust cloud my wagon was throwing up. Incredibly, Penny and her team had closed the gap, coming up on the left, her lead horses almost even with my back left wheel.

Damn! She'd slipped up behind me and taken the inside lane.

I whirled back to the front and slapped the reins against the horses again, hoping for more speed. Ahead, the first turn loomed, and I pulled the team left, guiding them into the top of the "U," the horses and wagon slowing slightly as they made the turn.

To my left, Penny and her Plum Crazy Purple B wagon appeared, turning tighter, edging ahead, finishing the turn ahead of me. Her purple hat flew off and her brown hair streamed in the wind. Shooting a look of triumph at me, Penny let out a blood-curdling yell. "Yee-hawww!"

Within seconds, I was eating her dust. Up ahead, smoke from the smoke bomb trailed from the wagon's rear.

Damn! In my heart, I knew I'd never catch her. Maybe she had the fastest team, I didn't know. But I did know she was terrific with horses.

I wished she hadn't yelled "Yee-hawww" at me.

Twenty feet ahead, she swung the team to the left, guiding them into the last long leg of the "U." As she skidded through the turn, her left front wagon wheel wobbled momentarily, then it wobbled again. Violently.

What the—?

Something had broken. Oblivious, Penny lashed the reins again, urging the horses out of the turn. Down at the wobbling wheel, the axle was no longer straight, but bent. It had broken. But not completely.

Penny hadn't seen the wobbling wheel. She didn't know she was in trouble.

Any second now and the axle spindle could snap like a toothpick and the wheel would fly off. The left front corner of the wagon would plow into the dirt and the buckboard would tumble and flip, spilling Penny forward.

She'd be run over by the wagon!

Slapping the reins hard, I turned my horses early, leaving the track, cutting well across the infield, angling to intercept Penny.

Ahead, the wheel continued to wobble, wobbling more now than ever before.

How the stupid wheel managed to stay on this long, I didn't know— "Damn you, don't break!" I yelled.

Lashing the reins, yelling at the horses, we roared forward, closing the gap, catching up to her in seconds, veering to parallel her. I shouted my lungs at her, hoping she could hear me over all the racket. "Penny!"

Penny fired an angry glance at me, knowing I'd taken a short cut, sure I was cheating, trying to win. She lashed the reins again, yelling, urging her horses forward. The grandstands and finish line were coming up fast.

I did the same, staying even with her, the two wagons thundering along side by side separated by only three feet. "Penny!"

She turned and stared at me, as if I had lost my mind.

"Stop!"

She shook her head, frowning.

Below her, the axle spindle splintered, barely holding.

There wasn't time for her to bring the team of horses to a stop.

There wasn't time for anything.

The wheel was coming off!

For God's sake, Penny, please trust me for once in your life. "Jump!"

Something came into Penny's eyes. As if in slow motion, she dropped the reins, stepped up on the seat, then leaped toward me, her hair flying.

Below her, the wagon wheel popped loose and shot into the air, narrowly missing Penny's legs, bounding a dozen feet high. Simultaneously, the axle plowed into the ground. The wooden buckboard disintegrated, flipping, smashing, tearing loose from the wagon tongue.

I raised my arms and caught Penny, wrapping my arms around her, pulling her into me tightly.

Overhead, the gyrating iron-rimmed wagon wheel was falling—straight for us!

I reared violently backwards, flipping the two of us—ass over teakettle—into the canvas-covered wagon bed.

Beyond our feet, the flying wagon wheel smashed down, busting the wooden seat to smithereens, then ricocheted away. The wagon careened wildly as our horses panicked, turning into the infield away from the wreckage of the other wagon.

They could flip us over, galloping full out!

Instinctively, I'd dropped the reins when I'd caught Penny. No telling where they were now. Inside the bouncing, bucking wagon, I struggled to free myself from Penny.

Suddenly, our horses slowed. Looking through the canvas opening,

I saw Joe Simpson riding beside the lead horses, a few reins taut in his right hand. "Whoa! Whoa!"

Good old Joe.

The clattering wagon rolled to a stop. It seemed oddly quiet, except inside my chest my heart was thumping like a bass drum.

I looked down at Penny, supporting herself on her elbow beside me. A warm glow flooded my body. Thank God she'd heard me telling her to jump. I didn't want to think about her lying under that wreck back there. Weakly, I lay back down beside her. "You all right?"

She snuggled into my arms, and looked up at me. Her freckled face was white, her eyes wide, as if she'd just now realized what nearly had happened. "Thanks for saving my life."

I didn't reckon as how I'd saved her life. "I'm just real glad you weren't hurt. Thanks ... for trusting me."

She slipped her right arm around me, pulling herself tighter against my body, her head beside mine, her brown hair tickling my cheek. "I've always trusted you, Frank. I love you."

She loved me?

I wasn't sure what to say, so I said, "Yeah?"

She pulled back, wrinkling her bunny nose in disgust. "And you owe me twenty dollars."

I blinked, my mind spinning. "What?"

The corners of Penny's wide mouth curled upward impishly and her long brown eyelashes lowered, veiling a mysterious sparkle within the depths of her eyes. "I didn't jump until after I crossed the finish line."

I felt a grin forming slowly on my face. My left hand was resting on her waist. The soft skin under her shirt stirred an image into my head. An image of me making love to Penny.

She loved me. I owed her twenty dollars. She loved me. I owed her twenty dollars. I didn't know whether to kiss her or reach for my billfold.

One thing I did know.

I loved her too.

Jameson Cole is a long-time member of RMFW who has been president, vice president, and nearly every other office the group has. Jim started RMFW's on-line critique groups. His novel, A Killing in Quail County, *won the Colorado Book Award for Best Novel. He served his country in the U.S. Army and is retired from a career as a National Defense Analyst with Lockheed Martin. Jim is married and lives in the Rocky Mountains near Woodland Park, Colorado.*

Losing the Light
by Rebecca S.W. Bates

We're all prisoners to the pull of the sun, the *Duranna* thought, streaking through the Oort Cloud as a beam of energy. An ice fragment tumbled away from her on its inbound fall.

She'd felt the homeward pull at Canopus, where the summons uplinked to her. The *Chudson* told her not to confirm—StarReach was lying. A recall now could only mean disaster, the *Chudson* had warned, and besides, it was more important for her to stay on schedule for Andromeda, instead.

But she was a *Duranna*. Her line of pilots never disconnected from the link to duty.

Outside the orbit of Saturn, she savored the song of the universe, the flow of stars in her veins of pure energy. Riding the beam coupled her with the cosmos, and she soared free of the human form. "Duranna *... come away with us...*" voices whispered, titillating her.

All too soon, drifting sparks and tingles reminded her of her corporeal being, and bit by bit, ensnared her essence into a glowing cocoon. Re-materialization stole her energy from her.

She shot into the asteroid belt as her brain-ship meld ran down to its inevitable end. The ship's hull slowly took shape from the glimmering stream around her, forming into a sleek bullet contour. *Duranna* tried to linger as a beam in the tentacled grip of the Transformation Device, but she couldn't hold onto singing stars much longer.

Her molecules spun. Hints of human shape lashed around the energy beam, within the hull. Past Mars, the song died, and the universe went cold, and she felt...

Nothing. The absence of light.

Neurons fired, and the last of her genetically engineered particles rearranged themselves. She was a form now, leashed to a titanic mass. But empty.

#

Matter transformation always left her body feeling more used up, and her mind momentarily disoriented. Despite her training and her enhanced DNA, she was still human—most of the time. The human form craved a spatial perception that didn't exist in the vacuum of her infinite playground.

Earth, reflecting more sunlight than she remembered, made her blink. Since the last time she'd seen the homeworld, clouds had grown thicker. Holes punched through the white shroud spotlighted brilliant ice fields.

Duranna turned away from Earth and took over from the shipboard program. She guided the ship, a 107 model, toward Luna Station hanging above her head like a string of bubbles. Behind the orbiting modules, the stark daytime surface of the moon filled most of the viewport, blinding her with its brightness. The 107 docked too hard against the moorings of its berth at the station.

A human's voice, no longer intelligible to her, burst over the speaker. It was a harsh gush of sounds compared to the stars' music. After a few clanging tugs at the hull, the outer hatch opened with a bang, jarring the Transformation Device, which held her torso with a few flickering remnants of light. A tech floated inside and launched himself toward her.

Duranna recognized fear on his face, and yes, maybe a bit of loathing, too. She'd seen it many times before. The unknown was what really frightened traditional humans when they came face to face with an embodied StarReach pilot.

The tech pulled a chip the size of a thumbnail out of his toolbox and held it up for her to inspect. She moved the lead weight of her head in a painful nod of approval, and he quickly inserted the chip into her cranial access.

"Is that better?" Now she could understand him. "Welcome back. Did you experience any difficulties on your trip?"

"Why the summons?" she asked instead, her new voice snapping to mask her own fear. StarReach wanted to retire her. "Why the rush?"

"Malfunction, ma'am." He went about his business, touching a sequence of pads, activating the release sequence. "You've experienced excessive sparking after transformation—"

"There's nothing wrong with my ship."

"If we don't take care of it right away, we could have an emergency situation. I'd say it's about time this old 107 came in for a refit." All the while, he worked without looking her in the eye. As if there were something not quite human about Duranna.

Her facial muscles twitched.

"The *Bra'er* and the *Eltsinoh* never made it back," the tech added. "People are questioning whether or not we should travel in space at all if we have to do it this way. With so many losses we've suffered lately, even the boss is getting nervous."

That would explain her summons.

#

By the time Duranna reached the boss's office in the burrows of Eagle City, she felt more like a spinning nebula than a human form. It was no simple task to adapt to this shape after skimming through space as a burst of energy. With each transformation, she needed more time to readjust.

Trume, the director of StarReach, limped out of a holo of a nighttime city hive. Extending a pale hand from the folds of a cloak, he was a tired-looking version of the young spitfire she'd first met fifty standard years ago. "Ah, Captain Duranna," he whispered, clasping her hand in a cold grip. "Welcome home."

"Thank you, sir. It's always a pleasure to return to Eagle City." The lie was a formality, but she knew the game.

"Good." Two slings dropped from the ceiling and caught them before Duranna tripped and fell.

"Once you're settled in your suite," the director continued, "you'll have the rest of today to, ah, relax." He twisted the cloak's clasp about his throat, and Duranna wondered if his discomfort was entirely physical. "Would you like a refreshment?" he added.

"I don't need one."

He chuckled and swung around to the food server, which dispensed two bulbs of amber liquid. "Sometimes we don't know what's best for us," he said, handing one to her. He lifted the other to his mouth.

She grunted, then followed his lead and sipped. She hated being a game-player, but how could she resist the engineering? The burning liquid startled her at first. Soon she relaxed and enjoyed the effect of the numbing fire in her throat. A memory tweaked at her of a moon bar filled with pilots drinking and bragging about their runs—*Bra'er* and *Tinacha*, among others. Pilots, all of them, sharing their passion with each other. She hadn't communed with anyone for a long, long time. The place was probably gone by now, she chided herself, turning her attention back to Trume.

"The docs always say that after transformation you should drink plenty of fluids." He set his bulb in a holder and watched her closely. His gaze drifted up to the peak of her bald head. "Tomorrow you'll report for a medical evaluation."

"Medical? There's nothing wrong with me."

His lengthy silence told her he didn't agree. "Still," he said finally, "you must remember it's a safety precaution for a pilot who's been out on as many runs as you."

"Is that why you called me back early? For a medical?"

He scowled and asked instead, "Do you know how many settlers you've transported altogether in your career?"

She shrugged and handled her bulb as cautiously as if someone had handed her a piece of cometary debris. "I don't keep count."

"We do. You're close to holding the record, which was set by the *Bra'er*."

She could easily believe it, but she'd soon surpass her colleague's record. Trume knew that.

"Reach has made a great deal of profit off of the Duranna line," he said. "Hundreds of years ago, we engineered your original for suitability to the brain-ship meld..."

His voice took on a hypnotic quality, as if he tried to lull her into relaxing. She felt numb, weighted down by body mass.

He droned on. "It was easier to clone your original than design a new one. Clones are easier to train, given their genetic propensity."

A tingle coursed through her, both similar to and different from the highs from sailing with the stars.

"Our clients are willing to invest life fortunes for a chance to establish colonies on new worlds. Fortunately for our enterprise, that old pioneering spirit won't be bred out." Trume paused, and the corners of his lips turned down. "But we've had a rash of losses lately, and business has dropped almost seventy percent."

She felt dizzy.

"We've lost six pilot-ships in the last year," he continued. "Each one of those ships costs as much as the cloning and training of ten new TD pilots."

"Your ships are useless without the pilots."

His eyes flashed as icy blue as the fires of Sirius. "And without passengers, you pilots are unnecessary. Our clients are afraid. If ships can disappear after debarkation, it's only a matter of time before one of them vanishes with a full load of passengers still aboard. The passenger rate is falling off sharply."

"*Bra'er*, *Eltsinoh* and who else have disappeared?"

He studied her with pity in his eyes, then spoke so low and quickly that she almost missed the names. "The *O'Willet*, the *Flenry*, the

Borsonk'v, and the *Tinacha*."

Damn. She slumped lower in her sling. All of them had logged as many, if not more, transits as she.

"We think it's the transformation process itself that's causing the problem," he continued quickly. "It's a risky business, this matter conversion, and we don't yet know all the long-term side effects."

He rambled on about the subtle loss of mass after each acceleration to lightspeed travel. However, Duranna was thinking about her six lost colleagues, all of them reduced to nothing more than a memory. Or perhaps a cosmic fragment.

"...for immigrants," Trume was saying, "the mass loss is minimal because they simply don't go through transformation often enough to make a difference. But for pilots who fly as much as you do, the accumulated effect of mass loss eventually makes that pilot ... er, lose mental control of the ship."

"We're going crazy?"

"I wouldn't put it exactly that way, but there seems to be a relationship between those who've disappeared and the number of their transformations."

A quake of uneasiness rippled through Duranna. She remembered the doubts she'd felt long ago when she was a trainee. Almost half of her class eliminated itself because of complete mental collapse. Back then, she'd reminded herself that such a flaw had never happened to any of the Durannas. In fact, this particular Duranna had adapted to transformation better than the other surviving members of her class. It had only taken her half a dozen attempts before she learned how to remain conscious during the procedure. Half a dozen more before she controlled the nose bleeds, blurred vision and mental disorientation that usually followed.

"Let me go back out there," she said, trying to rise, "and I'll find out what happened to them." Gravity pinned her down, and a sharp pain stabbed through her head. He'd drugged her drink!

"I'm afraid not," he said. "We need your ship. We have six trainees and no ships to meld them with."

She dropped the half-full drink and pushed herself up onto shaky legs despite the pounding in her head. "You can't take my ship away from me. It's *me*. Without it, I'm nothing. Without me, it's nothing."

"Of course, of course," he said in a soft, placating voice, as soft as his limp hands, which he tried to hide in the folds of his city cloak. "We thought you might object."

"Hunnhh." She blinked with surprise and new understanding. He was trying to tell her that the next Duranna, probably nearing termination in the training labs right now, was *better* than she was. StarReach wanted to refit her ship for the new clone.

Trume cleared his throat and groped inside his cloak. "Here, this will show you everything you need to know." He withdrew a mica-thin slate, splattered with color, and tossed it in a slow, curving arc. Her fists opened involuntarily to catch it. She wondered what had been added to her drink bulb to dull her resistance. "Use the red-orange-yellow sequence."

She took a step backwards and stumbled. Staring at the instrument resting in one palm, she thought that this was another diversion from some larger truth.

"Go on, try it."

It was a curious palette containing different colored circles, unlike anything she'd seen on her last visit here. "What is it, really?"

He nodded at it. "You'll see."

Hesitantly, she reached with her other hand, stretching her fingers, those awkward tentacles of the corporeal form, over the device. She looked back at him. His face leered at her, his thoughts clear. She couldn't adapt anymore, he was thinking. *Damn him*! She stabbed at the red area. A slight tickle responded in her fingertips, and she moved quickly to the orange, then yellow colors.

The room filled with red like the fires of Betelgeuse burning to its end.

Duranna sucked in her breath and jerked away from the colored pads as if they'd stung her. A voice crooned at her, a warm voice, and despite herself, she slumped back into the security of her sling chair. The city hive on the wall screen disappeared, and in its place was a red-black roil of clouds. No, they were waves. She could even feel the tingle of their spray on her cheeks.

Duranna! someone whispered in a siren's whisper, like the voices she'd heard riding the beam sunward.

She stared, transfixed, at the screen. No, the screen had disappeared, and only the cloud wave remained. No, it wasn't a wave but a nebula spinning its gases, shaping and re-shaping them, compressing... Now she felt its warmth.

Duranna, sang a voice to her from within the nebula. A figure emerged from its depths. A woman, walking from nothing, from nowhere, into the room. She wore a long, flowing robe of her own hair, and she glided closer, close enough to allow her face to be seen.

It was herself! A Duranna with hair.

She reached out to touch the glittering hair but couldn't make contact. *She wasn't real.* Then she understood she was seeing a virtual version of an earlier Duranna—maybe the original herself.

Duranna, the unreal woman whispered. *Your body fails you. Now comes the time...*

She squirmed. Felt the back of the sling stick to her naked scalp. She had known. But she'd ignored the signals out of a sense of duty.

If you accept your termination as an interstellar pilot of the transformation type...

Duranna felt the soundless scream of her vocal chords. *All I know is being the ship!*

They will refit you and give you everything you want at Four Seasons, the colony for retired pilots...

She was a pilot, an active pilot. All she wanted was the stars.

If you refuse... Her instructions dangled amidst bursts of sparks charging the air. The cloud wave swirled, lashed, and the image of the woman faded. A terrain of blizzard white swept against the remnants of domed cities. Even inside, a sensation of cold swept through her, set her bones to rattling. She felt the sting of Earth's glacier fields and frozen seas. Their leaden weight pulled on her human shape as she fought for a gutter to call her own. A fine treatment for uncooperative employees.

No, she thought, struggling for her voice, hearing only a hissing sound ringing through her head. *Being the* Duranna *is all I know.*

#

She awoke later, feeling the sense of panic that usually prevailed over her human manifestation. This time she didn't know where she was. Not even who she was. Was it possible that she'd already been transported to the labs, that the refitting had begun, that she was doomed to live out the rest of her days in the prison of exile?

Her brain throbbed. Her throat burned. Muscles ached in her chest, muscles she never knew she had. She was lying in a bed somewhere, in a blazing white room where liquids dripped through clear tubing from an overhead network. With tentative fingers, she reached up from the crinkly, metallic blanket to touch her naked scalp.

She started to sit up against the forces holding her down. Movement was easier now. Must be adjusting to gravity. Didn't *want* to adjust. Wasn't ready for rehab, no matter what they dripped into her veins. She'd never be ready.

A monitor screamed warning bleeps at her movement. She swung her legs out from the bindings of the blanket, and a tray of vials crashed to the floor. The room swayed, but she pushed herself up onto her feet anyway. Yanked the hook-ups from her access. What were they feeding her to make her feel this woozy?

The door blinked open and two moon-bred Amazons rushed into the room. They blocked her exit, and she scooped up the dangling, dripping tubes. Pointing them as if they were miniature laser sticks stopped the two short of grabbing her. *Must be damned powerful stuff in this brew.*

"Get me my clothes," she snapped at one of them. "What's wrong, are you deaf, man? Move!"

The woman she'd called a man exchanged a meaningful glance with her compatriot. They shrugged, then with one swift step, they surrounded Duranna, lifted her up and strapped her onto a platform hastily produced from the wall.

Before she could protest further, the doors opened again, and Trume glided in, his cloak swirling about him. "Well, Captain, I see you're feeling better."

"What do you mean by confining me this way? Am I under arrest?"

"Why, no," he said, lowering his eyes to watch his feet trace patterns on the gleaming white floor.

"Then I demand to be released at once. How dare you treat me this way?"

"Regrettably, we can't allow your release."

"Why not?"

"You know the answer to that. Refitting is for your protection."

"Is it? Maybe it's for your protection. What is it you're trying to hide from me?"

He gave her a wistful smile, then nodded at one of the Amazons, who slid open cubby doors and pulled out coils of tubes and new vials of a sparkling, clear liquid.

Her heart raced. A sick feeling weighed at her stomach. This was more than a matter of refitting her for retirement and the ship for upgrade. They'd been lying to her all the way from the summons she'd received at Canopus. Maybe before that. Whatever they were keeping from her had something to do with those lost pilots. More than that, it was to do with lost business. Lost revenue. Lost ships. They feared truth and would hide it from the worlds.

She watched the Amazon move heavily across the room with untangled tubes dripping from one arm. Trume hung onto a handhold built into the wall near the foot of her platform and waited. For what? Duranna squirmed against her bindings as the moon woman reached her side and moved toward her cranial hook-up.

No! Fury built within her, spreading, rushing, like the gases of an expanding star. Heat...

If they completed the drug treatment, Duranna would never be able to control her own body again, let alone her ship.

The Amazon dangled the tubes as she guided one of them closer. Slower. In slow motion. The weight of gravity, even as reduced as the moon's, slowed her movements.

Bindings held Duranna fast, and all she could do to struggle against her fate was shrink into herself. Wish herself away from here, away from her helplessness.

No!

She'd never been helpless a day in her life. That life flashed through her mind, a mind filled with enhanced genes, generationally altered. Feeling began to flood the empty shell of her body, and she directed its fire through her veins. She owned her thoughts, channeled her being, controlled every corpuscle flowing through her body, as never before she'd been able to control. All of her years of training, of transformation, had given her this moment of release.

"I don't understand it," the Amazon whispered.

Faintly aware. A blur of movement at Duranna's side as she focused inward. Inward... Following the flow of ... blood ... streaming...

"It's administering, but..."

"She *looks* sedated," said Trume.

"But her heart rate is accelerating. She's going into arrest."

Scuffling sounds around her. Something trickled. Something screamed at her. Resistance slipped. Slipping ... into a stream of stars...

The particles in her body fell away one by one. She commanded them. She could arrange them where she wished. Build them in different patterns.

She no longer needed the ship to do it for her.

"Give her more!" Trume shouted.

"It'll kill her."

"...Get her into suspension ... stop this. Now!"

Movement. Duranna felt the flow tug at her. Faster. She, plastered to the platform, against racing motion. Cloaks, blankets, tubings flapped around her. Faster. Farther. White flashing past. She shifted under the straps holding her down. Began to flow like a liquid spiral.

Trume's voice pierced the ether. "Stop this once and for all, or it's my ass."

He knew, Duranna thought. This. The unknown.

"She'll never make it to the chamber," a moon woman shouted.

"She has to," Trume said, gasping. "Can't ... take this step..."

"What's she...?"

"It's too late."

"She's *glowing*!"

Trume whimpered. "What have we created?"

Duranna, a burst of energy, streamed out from under the bindings, off the platform, past the human faces awash with horror, weighted down with gravity. Leaving the humans behind, she spurted down the corridor. A bolt of pure energy, she shot out into a domed park, up the side of a tree, splintering branches with her charged passage. She reached the domed ceiling with a supersonic boom as alarms blared and seals slid into place, but not before she fanned out through the jagged break.

Out.

Into space.

Luna Station glinted against black eternity. The 107 would be laced with construction lattices, but she didn't need it anymore. What *Duranna* hadn't known until now was that she could transform without the device. *Bra'er* and the rest had done it. They'd all found a way to break free...

Trume had suspected. Had feared.

Her energy self turned away from the glaring moon, its child's space station, its Earth cradle. Turned away to follow the next path, her true path.

Duranna! Voices titillated from beyond. No longer a prisoner to this sun, she streamed away.

Rebecca Bates grew up in Turkey and Brazil and eventually settled in Boulder, Colorado, where she raised three daughters and taught Spanish. She now writes full time and has published several SF and fantasy short stories, most recently in Future Syndicate. *Her SF novella will appear in* Infradead *in 2009. She has also published a suspense novel,* The Drowning of Chittenden.

A Long Way
by Susan G. Fisher

Pops had a new love. At least I hoped he did. After being out every night for two weeks, it was time for him to share her with me, his daughter in search of a new mother. His paperback book formed a Berlin wall between us at the breakfast table. "Science fiction?" I asked as I pulled it down. "Who gave you that book?"

He fanned pages with notes written sideways in every margin. The sleeves of his navy-blue sweatshirt, embossed with our company logo, bunched up at his elbows. His arms shook almost imperceptibly. He had goose-pimples on his tanned skin, as if it were the coldest day of the year. "I'm glad you asked, Lynet," he said.

I had so many questions. Something told me the answers were all the same. Why had he taken a leave of absence a month ago from the MIC, the Milwaukee Insurance Company, where he had headed up the actuary department for thirty years? And what woman had distracted him so much that he stopped training for the 2008 Milwaukee Marathon?

He must really be smitten. I liked the fact that she obviously wasn't a runner; that was for me and Pops alone. I imagined her wiping melted chocolate off her fingers from the cookies waiting for us when we returned from work. I couldn't wait to share long talks with her in my bedroom at night. It was okay that he had stopped reading the Wall Street Journal, substituting *Between Planets* by Robert Heinlein. She must be out of this world.

Pops wasn't talking yet. "Earth to astronaut Harimann Hause," I said.

He folded down the top corner of page sixty-four and put the book face-down on the antique oak table top. Creases formed in its spine. I noticed black smudges on the tips of his fingers from ink printed on cheap paper. Why hadn't he at least bought the hardback to add to his library?

"I'm studying up on the concept of paying it forward," he said. "Heinlein was the first to talk about it."

Another of his endless philosophical fascinations. If I didn't get to my point, he'd talk on endlessly about his. "How much longer before you introduce us?" I asked. I checked my Blackberry for the time. It was only seven a.m. on this 102-degree first Monday in August, three hours until I was scheduled to present at our monthly staff meeting. From my five-year analysis of life insurance claims, I would make a bold proposal. They'd agree we had to raise our premiums by ten percent to increase our profit margins. Too many people were dying. They'd promote me, putting me on track to replace Pops years from now when he retired.

Pops cleared his throat and looked at me. What I saw was a sixty-four-year-old, athletic, brilliant man with pleading in his walnut-brown eyes. "I always wanted to see the Rocky Mountains," he said.

His new love interest must be a western gal. "If you're thinking about the Denver Marathon, forget it," I said. "It's only two weeks after ours, and frankly, you're in no shape for either." We had agreed to target a time of three hours eleven minutes this year, our personal best. If we ran in Denver, we'd be lucky to achieve three hours fifty-six minutes at an altitude that was five thousand feet higher. Unacceptable.

We had run in Milwaukee every October for thirty-two years, matching stride for stride, exactly two feet apart, letting no one push between us. It was as if an invisible chain stretched between our shoulders the whole while our five-foot eleven-inch frames pumped toward the red and orange leaves in Veteran's Park. We both sported the physique of every distance runner: long muscles, stiff torso, lean legs, and skinny arms.

"You don't understand," he said, tapping the upside-down book with his index finger.

I didn't. We needed to stick to the original plan, the one he had devised for us the year after Mom died when I was ten. Six hours and forty-nine minutes that first race. I still threw up every time and had to be helped to the car, but I always finished.

"Colorado," he said. He got up and prepared fruit for his breakfast, slicing mangoes and popping the seeds out of a pomegranate. They stained his hands the same colors as the autumn maples along Lake Michigan. What had happened to the daily banana that kept his runner's muscles from cramping?

I poured more Vermont maple syrup on my toaster waffles. "Come on, have some of these," I urged. I watched him get a four-liter container of protein powder out of the cupboard and mix two scoops with water in one of our largest glasses. He gulped down the white glop but had to stop because he was choking.

I abandoned my breakfast, walked over to him, and rubbed his back until he seemed calm. "Take a break; I'll be back in ten," I said. I showered, cut the tags from a white silk blouse I had bought on sale at Neiman Marcus, and donned my grey pin-stripe suit.

When I carried my cordovan leather brief case into the kitchen, Pops was reading that book again. He was eating blueberries now. A purple ring soaked into the oak table under the bowl. He stirred the berries, took a bite, and got that unfocused look, as if he were in ecstasy at the skins popping, at the taste of slightly-tart fruit-flesh slipping over his tongue.

After he finished chewing, he looked at me. "I quit my job," he said.

I dropped the briefcase on a ladder-back chair. "You didn't," I said. "When?"

He moved the bowl around and around until curved stains covered his side of the table. "I called the company president late Friday afternoon. You had already left the office."

Pops knew where I went every Friday, to visit my mother's grave. What he didn't know was that I took the long way home, staring into my aunt's lighted kitchen window where she and her daughters prepared dinner together, envying my cousins the family life they took for granted.

"But why?" I looked at his face and noticed lines that hadn't been there before. What if this wasn't about a woman?

He swallowed. "Lynet, I need more time," he said.

I led him outside to Mom's front porch swing where he could smoke his burled briarwood pipe. It would calm him. I slid one of Mom's hand-stitched quilts under my butt and legs to protect me against slivers. We never got around to sanding and oiling the weathered teak boards. Pops was shivering. I pulled another quilt up around his neck and snuggled up against him. "Now tell me," I said. "What's going on?"

He put his arm around my shoulder. "I'm so sorry," he said.

His voice sounded as scratchy as Mom's old Christmas records, Bing Crosby and Perry Como. He had been getting dizzy, he said. A lot. The doctors did all the tests. The diagnosis was an inoperable tumor in his brain.

He stopped talking, as if his voice box refused to push out one more word. I could hear myself breathing as I waited for him to say he was just kidding, a cruel joke. He touched his hand to my white silk collar. It'd leave fingerprints, I thought. I'd have to hand-wash it tonight. After we sat on that porch swing and watched the fireflies. After I breathed in the peaty scent of his tobacco, like I had been doing my whole life.

He started talking again. He didn't have long enough to make up for past mistakes, he said. Like letting me become so like him. Like cheating me out of the adventure that would send me crashing into the unknown. He had always longed for that. He was sorry he had never told me before now. I noticed that Mom's rosebushes needed pruning.

Then he was trying to explain about Heinlein.

I wanted the music from old holiday albums to block out his voice. *Should auld acquaintance be forgot?* That was the last song on every holiday album. Every year on Thanksgiving, I got the records from the basement and played them. Pops loved them, too. He and I always danced to *White Christmas* across the hardwood kitchen floor.

"Paying it forward means you get something from someone but you don't give anything in return right away." My cell phone was ringing in the kitchen. "Instead of paying them back, you do something for someone else in the future." He asked me if I understood.

"I should answer that," I said, before running inside. My assistant was on the line.

"Excuse me," he said. It came out sounding like *exsme.* The Blackberry needed a new battery. He wondered where the report was for today's meeting. He had to make copies.

"I can't talk to you now." I didn't wait for his response. I turned off the phone, walked to the front screen door, and looked at a spider picking his way across the wire mesh toward a web spotted with dewdrops.

"Where were you, all those nights?" I asked Pops.

He had gone to a Heinlein Society meeting, he said, where he met Kiya. They had a lot to talk about. He should have been home talking to me.

"Like what?" I asked. "And who's Kiya?"

Pops lifted his feet to the seat of the porch swing and put his head on the arm. Kiya had come to Milwaukee for the Heinlein forum, Pops said. They had gone out for coffee, sharing their troubles. When it became obvious they could help each other, they had made a deal. Kiya would take care of us.

I flicked my index finger against the wire mesh of the screen, trying to dislodge the spider. "And what is this Kiya needing help with?" I asked.

Pops sprang upright as if a surge of electricity had jolted him. "He told me all about the Rockies: the jagged peaks you can't take your eyes off, the thrill of seeing a moose so close he could trample you if he chose."

Not a woman, I thought. A man with a problem. An intruder. I watched the spider freeze in place as I opened the door and stepped onto the porch. Kneeling next to the swing, I took my father's hand.

He turned his head toward me. "You and Kiya, take me to the mountains," he whispered. The swing rocked like a cradle.

#

Pops deteriorated so rapidly that within two weeks he couldn't get to the bathroom by himself. On August 20th, I moved him to the skilled nursing wing of St. Johns on the Lake.

Pops must have telephoned Kiya, because he met my Toyota Prius with a wheelchair. He was unobtrusive about it, but I could tell he was checking me out as he settled Pops back against a cushion and flipped the foot rests down. I walked around the car and looked down on him. He was about five inches shorter than me, and at least ten years younger. "I don't want your help," I said.

"All the same," he answered, in a bass voice that reverberated like a tympani drum, no matter that he spoke quietly. "Your father and I have an agreement." His crew cut, black as mica, topped a cinnamon-colored face dominated by a squat nose. He wore a blue shirt the color of Lake Michigan way out where the sailboats flew their spinnakers on their way to Mackinac.

Pops patted Kiya on the arm and asked me to go park the car. Five minutes later, I found them in a ten-by-twelve room. Kiya and I transferred Pops out of the wheelchair when his legs buckled under him. The bed was too narrow. How could he possibly be comfortable? He went right to sleep.

"Good time for a training run," Kiya said. He lounged against the turquoise and purple wallpaper as if he were waiting for a bus. A silver embossed rodeo buckle adorned the slim waist of his form-fitting blue jeans. From under his boot-cut hems, worn leather cowboy boots poked out, unpolished except for the silver tips on the toes.

I sat in the wheel chair and crossed my arms. "It's none of your business what I do," I said. "You might as well leave, because I'm the one who will be caring for Pops."

He shrugged. "All kinds of reasons to do something."

I stayed put, and so did he. For two days.

#

On the third night, I went home exhausted after lights-out at St. Johns. By then, Kiya had taken to sitting in the hallway just outside Pops' door, wood chair-back leaning against the wainscoting, front chair legs wavering a foot off the floor. I had no idea where he lived. Maybe he rented a guest room at St. Johns; he was always there.

Something happened when I returned the next day, some kind of unspoken truce. He showed me how to use the draw-sheet to shift Pops every couple of hours. I waited for my resentment to surface, but all I felt was grateful. I watched him put just a little cream of wheat on a spoon and wipe Pops' lips in between each small mouthful. Pops smiled up at him.

"Thank you," I said. He offered his favorite snack, peanuts dropped into a paper cup of Dr. Pepper. I found I liked the sweet smell and the way the fizz wet my cheeks. We settled into a routine as if we had been taking care of Pops together all our lives.

About three in the afternoon, Kiya faced down a scrubs-attired nurse who came to check Pops' blood pressure. He wasn't rude about it, just said "nope," and ushered her to the door. I heard her suggest she come back later.

"We three," he said, "are doing just fine on our own." He seemed taller after that.

We went to have coffee in the dining room while Pops was napping. Kiya chided me for spending every waking moment at St. Johns. "You need to take care of yourself," he said. When I thought about me, all I saw was a blackness advancing like the mother of all twisters. I shook my head. He got up to refill his cup.

When he came back to our table, I asked him why he had taken on this job. Pops could have paid him some huge amount before we came to St. Johns, despite that mumbo-jumbo about paying it forward.

"Heinlein," he said. "That first meeting, when I met your father, I had come from Colorado to see what it was all about." I protested, insisted it didn't make any sense that he would stay on to care for a man he had only recently met. "It's my decision," he said.

Then I remembered Pops' comment, that Kiya had his troubles too. I asked him about that. "It's my sister," he said. "Wyn's the horse trainer on our family ranch." Without her, he explained, the family business would fail. Kiya needed me to talk to her. Because I understood about family loyalty, about business, about making a living.

I didn't mention that I had taken unpaid leave from the MIC. How could I walk the corridor every day when someone else was sitting in Pops' office chair? To change the subject, I asked where his name came from.

"Short for Wanikiya," he said. He seemed amused at the question. He pushed away from the table, stretched his cowboy boots out on an extra chair, and put his hands behind his head. His father had bestowed the name on him at puberty, he explained. Sioux custom. Sort of like a confirmation name in the Catholic religion.

"What does it mean?" I asked.

"You'll laugh," he said.

"Try me."

"Savior," he said. "It means savior."

I pulled wrinkles out of the tablecloth. "So you have a God complex or something?"

"Nope." He moved his cup and slurped black coffee from the saucer. "I'm just getting through this life, same as you."

#

On Labor Day morning, Pops felt like such a dead weight that I couldn't turn him. His mind was wandering again, but he responded to the Jean Naté I had spritzed on, like I did every morning. He knew it was me from the lemony smell. Kiya and I stooped down on opposite sides of the bed, reached under Pops to interlace our fingers, and lifted him.

I couldn't let go. It was as if we were fused together, all three of us. When I finally unknotted my fingers from his, Kiya straightened the blanket around Pops. I caught a whiff of my scent on Kiya's hands. It preceded him every time he came into the room to check on us that day. I sat in the wheelchair and watched Pops sleep.

That night the bed looked so much larger. Pops' bones seemed to be dissolving. When I touched him, it felt like I was sifting through ashes. He was lucid, though. He asked me to put Enya on the CD player, the *Pilgrim* track. I did and then knelt down beside him. "You have to eat to keep up your strength," I said.

He started crying. "I can't swallow," he rasped.

I looked up and down the hall, and spotted Kiya helping an EMT wheel out a gurney, the occupant's face entirely covered by an oxygen mask. It was the first time he had paid attention to any patient other than Pops. I rang the call bell. An Asian woman in pink scrubs came in and identified herself as the hospice nurse.

"It's time to let him go," she said. She put her arms around me, but I shrugged them off. How dare she?

I sat on the floor next to Pops, peeled an orange, squished segments into pulp and rubbed them on his lips. As he licked at the sticky residue through his smile, I sucked the sweetness off my own fingers. When we were both done, he spoke in almost his normal voice. "Take me to the Rockies," he said.

I looked up to see Kiya watching me from the doorway. "I'm hoping you'll tell him yes," he said. "Let him know it's okay to let go of this world and step into the next. Alone."

I couldn't.

I lashed out at him. "You'd do anything to get me to go to Colorado," I said.

Kiya came into the room and sat on the floor next to me, the yoke of his blue-and-white-striped cowboy shirt against the wall. "There's a lake I know," he said. Pops and I listened as he described a rugged canyon, with sounds of water lapping against shoreline just below rock cliff walls.

"That's the place I want to be," Pops said. Then he was asleep, snoring through a mouth open wide to capture every molecule of oxygen.

I had to go somewhere and feel normal again. I washed my hands at the little sink three steps from the bed, put on my sweater, and left. First I drove to our house, parked in the driveway, and studied Mom's lace curtains in all the windows. Pops' pipe still sat on the porch swing. I didn't get out of the Prius.

When I backed out, I headed toward the MIC building. I drove slowly past, then speeded up and turned toward the cemetery. "What should I do, Mom?" I asked the headstone. There was no reply. I made my way back to my car and drove my usual Friday night route, but it wasn't dark enough outside to see inside the windows of my aunt's house.

An hour and a half later, I was back at St. Johns. There was no sign of Kiya. I stroked Pops' head and he didn't respond. There would be no normal for me, ever again. Sitting on the floor beside him with a road atlas open on my lap, I described the route I'd take to Colorado: mostly Interstate 80, through cow-towns like Cheyenne and Laramie, then south to Estes Park, winding up to Trail Ridge Road in Rocky Mountain National Park, the top of the world, and down to Highway 34 all the way to Lake Granby, and then around that huge reservoir to tiny Monarch Lake. It was the place Kiya had talked about.

"It's a long way," I said, hoping that the trip would last forever, me and Pops alone together again. I remembered using those same exact words when we ran our first marathon together.

I had been ten years old, and, at ten miles in, I couldn't take another step. "I have to pee, Pops," I had panted; "I'll catch up." I had peeled off toward the row of porta-potties, but their semi-circular signs all read *occupied*. The letters were red. I went around back of one and vomited. After emptying my stomach, I backed away and lay down in the wet grass. Pops had to be a mile ahead by now. Sixteen-point-two miles to go, on my own. I had wiped my mouth with red and yellow leaves before I struggled to my feet, feeling woozy. When I got back to the road, Pops was there, reaching out for me. He had circled back. We held hands all the way across the finish line.

Now Pops was nearing the finish line of his life. "Don't come back for me this time," I whispered to his unconscious form. "I mean it. You go on to the next world without me. I'll catch up with you sometime." I promised him I'd carry what was left of his body with me until I found the right place to let it go, as well.

I was sitting in the wheelchair, my lined jean jacket covering my legs, when the hospice nurse checked Pops one last time. "He's gone," she said.

I knew.

"Take as long as you like," she told me. *What's to like about being alone?* I thought.

I stayed there all night. When they came to pick up Pops' body early the next morning, I left. After forty-two years of living in the same house, I couldn't remember how to get back to it. I sat in my Toyota on the side of a busy street, listening to Enya, trying to figure out where I was headed. The words of her song haunted me: *"Pilgrim it's a long way, to find out who you are."*

Somehow I made it home.

#

The next two days I spent closing up the house and waiting for the mortuary to call me so I could pick up the cremains. When I did, my suitcase was in the trunk of the Prius. Pops rode up front in the passenger seat, the eight-by-eight-by-four-inch teak container nestled in a cardboard box that had previously held a case of Pabst Blue Ribbon beer. It had always been brewed in Milwaukee, Pops had told me last year, but not anymore. I wondered if I was leaving for good, as well.

I hadn't called Kiya, and he had left me alone to do my grieving.

#

I found the lake all right. With a backpack surprisingly heavy from Pops' ashes, I made my way across the parking lot, signed in at the ranger's cabin, and set out along the north shore trail. Within ten minutes I spotted the bull moose and his cow wading into the water off the point. They were far enough away for their legs to look like black sticks silhouetted against the aspen yellow reflected in the water. They seemed like something from another planet: alien, but not dangerous. I stumbled through the scree field, not looking down, staring at the animals and superimposing the image of my Pops, his limbs drawn up against his body under white sheets.

The animals raised heads too heavy for their bodies and observed my progress, dewlaps dripping, weeds from the lake bottom hanging from their jaws. Then they melted back into the high brush of the marsh. I wiggled out of my pack and reached for the water bottle. My fingers brushed against the teak box. I shouted at it. "This wild enough for you, Pops?"

I strapped the pack on again and continued on the trail toward a towering rock wall. It was the kind of place where I could imagine a mountain lion crouching high above me, waiting to spring. Kiya would shoot it in mid-pounce, probably with a bow-and-arrow. I lifted my chin and scanned for movement. Nothing. One massive thunderhead crowned the cliff, outlined by an azure sky.

Pops was dead. I had nothing left. Except running.

That's when I decided I'd stay in Colorado and train for the Denver Marathon.

The wind kicked up a swirl of pine needles, stirring a scent of resin. Orange dominated the low brush, but above, a cascade of gold swirled through the black deadfalls of Ponderosa pines. The local paper said that the pines were killed by beetles, all of the mature ones anyway. The aspen trees were healthy, gleaming in the late afternoon sun. The only contrasting colors up high were dark blue-greens from the occasional blue spruce and the limey transparency of the few aspens yet unchanged.

The hill looked to me like the side of a volcano with flaming lava decimating everything in its path as it flowed toward the lake. I looked behind me. Sun glare glanced off of lake water so clear that, in the shadows of trees and immense boulders, I could see fish pointed upstream among the rocks on the sandy bottom. Thunder echoed across the canyon. Could it possibly be the right thing to do, leaving Pops alone to face such wildness for all eternity?

But he was the one who left me. How could he not be with me to run this next race?

I felt an overpowering rage then. This was the world Pops had forced me to leave my home for, and I had to face it alone. I took off my backpack, pulled the box out, opened the latches, and ripped open the thick plastic bag. Attacking the steep hillside, I pushed upward as far as I could until I was surrounded by orange and gold leaves quaking in down-gusts from clouds. They made rattling, crackling sounds like the fires of hell.

Holding the opaque white bag by its bottom, I shook Pops' cremains over the slope until bushes and low-hanging limbs and one clump of purple lupines were all covered with the grey tailings. This was all that was left of the man who had been my partner my whole life.

I slid all the way down, past the trail and to the boulders along the lakeshore, before I crumpled to the ground, empty plastic bag in hand. That's when a wailing started, so powerful I couldn't believe it could be coming out of my own body. The moose, the bears, the mountain lions, they could come and get me. Then I could stay here.

After what must have been hours, I stopped long enough to feel cold. My backpack had an extra fleece jacket in it. I looked up to see where I had left it. When I tried to move, I felt as stiff as if I were sixty-four, like Pops.

#

No, the lady at the registration table assured me, there was no way to get into the marathon the day of the race. All the slots had been assigned weeks ago.

As I turned away, I felt a hand across my shoulder. Kiya, a numbered vest tied across his tank top, held another one out to me in his other hand.

"This one's for you," he said. We sat on a grassy area and stretched out before we lined up in the middle of the pack, as if we had trained together all our lives.

"I don't know if I can do this," I said.

"You will anyway," he assured me.

A slim woman trotted over to us. Her face looked like his, with prominent cheekbones, wide-spread nostrils, and black eyes like midnight ponds. Her thick, straight hair barely touched her shoulders, with bangs almost hiding her thick eyebrows. She was taller than him, and slim, like a runner. "My sister Wyn," he said, with a nod in her direction. "I asked her to feed you fry bread tomorrow and show you around our ranch in the foothills."

Family. I couldn't think of any place I'd rather be right now.

The three of us jogged in place and scissored our arms to stay loose. The starting gun went off. It took five minutes before the front runners cleared the way enough for us to make any forward progress. We were still dancing around, bumping into people crowding around us. We heard cheering and clapping and the sound of rubber slapping against pavement as more and more runners reached their strides.

Kiya shouted at me. "You two go ahead. Don't let me slow you down. I'll find you when I cross the finish line."

Then Wyn and I were moving, matching step for step, her stride as long as mine although she was a couple inches shorter in height. She shouted at me over the noise of onlookers cheering us on. "You here to lecture me about staying on the ranch?"

I was gasping for breath already, desperately sucking in the thin air. "I'm so far away from home," I said, panting between each word. "Who am I to tell you anything?"

"Will you go back?" she asked. I stumbled, and she took my arm to steady me.

"I don't know," I said. But where else could I go? Why not stay here a while? Hunker down, close down, think about nothing, feel nothing. Our strides lengthened as the runners in front of us put more distance between us. I breathed deeply and struggled to find a rhythm.

"I rented a place in Denver," Wyn shouted. "You could crash there awhile." Her arms moved easily in rhythm with her body, while mine pumped up and down. I couldn't think of anything but the next step. She eased back to stay with me.

I hit the wall at twenty miles and stopped to throw up. She jogged in circles. "I can't go any farther," I said. She reached out to me.

We crossed the finish line together, holding hands.

Susan Fisher knew she wanted to write fiction by age six. After a lifetime of adventures, which included growing up as an Air Force brat, crewing on racing sailboats, training horses, traveling the world for her business career, and volunteering at a hospice, she had collected enough stories to begin. Four years ago, after her daughter suggested it was time, she retired and joined RMFW. Since then, she has written a novel and numerous short stories. She resides in Arvada, Colorado. A Long Way *is her first published story.*

Water Monster
by Mario Acevedo

"Are you sure this is going to mend things?" Chato the fairy asks.

"You got a better plan?" I reply.

"I'm really sorry about what happened," Chato says.

"Tell that to Leadpipe O'Brien," I say. Leadpipe is a troll over in Stator City. Not just a troll, but a made troll. Earns his living as a thumb breaker, a leg breaker, a wing breaker, a tentacle puller-offer. Don't get me started on what he'd do to a unicorn.

"Don't lay it all on me," Chato says. He's about the size of a mouse with a blur of wings holding him up. "You keep jumping to conclusions. I start telling you one thing, and then you go yeah, yeah, I get it, and screw up what I'm trying to tell you."

"Yeah, yeah, I get it." Fairies. They never shut up. I frown. "Seems as I remember it was your info on a centaur race that got me into this mess. Put everything down on Too Much Bourbon, a thoroughbred from Underground Kentucky. Can't lose." I quirk an eyebrow at Chato. He hates when humans do that.

Chato put a hand up to his face and turns his head. "You didn't let me finish. I was going to say..."

I wave him off. "Yeah, yeah, I get it."

Chato goes on, "I didn't tell you to borrow from Leadpipe. That's why you're in this mess."

"Yeah, yeah." I figured if I could've made a small fortune on that bet, I could've made a big fortune if I could get my hands on some real cash. Trouble was, I was all tapped out except for Leadpipe. Yeah, I could've made a fortune if the bet would've paid off. If that stupid centaur hadn't tripped on his two left feet and fallen on the racetrack.

My life seems more broken than usual, and I was hoping to use my winnings to fix things. Now if I can't pay Leadpipe, my life won't be the only thing that will need fixing.

I climb down the steps from the Greenville trolley station and emerge from under the awning. I walk down the trail to the beach. To my right, shops and cafés crowd against the pier. A jetty made of rocks and broken concrete extends beyond the pier like a long, crooked finger. The bright sun makes me glaze in sweat.

Chato hovers by my ear. The heat gets to him. His wings start to sputter. He buzzes to my shoulder and sits.

I whisk him off. "No mooching rides. You wanna come along, you gotta fly the rest of the way."

I carry a cigar box. It's got all the cash I could scrape into a pile. A very small pile.

I've pawned everything I owned. And a lot I didn't. But it went to a good cause. Keeping Leadpipe from breaking my ass and everything connected to it. I'd even dropped by Evil-lyn at her beauty shop—Medusa's Eye of the Beholder—and helped myself to her till when she wasn't looking.

I'd sold my crystal oracle (and lost all the remaining minutes of my calling plan). My last call had been to Leadpipe when I asked for more time to collect the money. Apparently, he was in a cash flow jam as well and told me he'd forgive the difference on one condition.

A big condition.

A huge condition.

I'd have to deliver the money myself. That meant crossing Enron Lagoon to Leadpipe's house on Pandora Island.

There's only one way to cross Enron Lagoon. Safely, that is. In an armored launch protected with flamethrowers and electro harpoons.

See, the water monster lives in Enron Lagoon. I've never seen the water monster but I've heard stories. Make you barf and piss-your-pants stories.

I had said to Leadpipe, "I can't afford the ticket for the launch crossing, not unless it comes out of what I owe you."

"Like hell," Leadpipe had replied. "I'm cutting you plenty of slack. What are you, a were-weasel?"

So I'm stuck making the crossing in whatever I can float across the lagoon.

What's in it for Leadpipe? Word through the grapevine is that he and his buddies will be watching me cross and taking bets to see if I make it. What about the cash in my cigar box? I've heard that if the water monster gets me, the money is a business loss.

And me? I'm the entertainment.

Trolls. I hate trolls.

Chato tells me, "Not to worry, boss. I got us a ringer."

"Yeah, yeah." I got plans of my own.

"Don't leave without me," Chato says and flies off in the direction of the jetty.

The tide is out and the sun ripples along the beach. The air smells like stagnant water, dead fish, and pirate ship bilge. I make my way across the tidal flat toward a bunch of cabins that stand on mossy stilt-like pilings. Pebbles crunch beneath my moccasins.

I head toward one long cabin that's closest to the jetty. A gondola rests in a shallow pool of tide water by one of the pilings.

Here's my plan. I have the reputation as a weapons expert based on my service with the Magic Musket Rangers during the Succubus-Gnome War. What I don't tell people is that I served with the rangers as a clerk. And I spent the war in Port Silver as part of the defense force against aerial dragon attack.

Which never happened.

Thanks to the presence of our regiment of rangers. Or the anti-saurian hex put in place by the Warlock Brigade. Or the protective spell cast by the Witch Marines.

Confidentially, what kept the dragons away weren't us rangers, or the hexes, or the spells, but the batteries of radar-directed 90 millimeter anti-aircraft guns.

When I wasn't repelling dragon attacks that never happened, or pulling guard duty, or mopping floors and scrubbing toilets, I kept busy unloading supplies on the black market. The locals didn't have much cash, but the women offered plenty of tail. Gecko babes are freaky that way.

I traded my skills as an entrepreneur with my fellow rangers, and they in turn showed me how to blow things up.

I reach the cabin. I climb up the ladder and onto the deck. There's a lock on the door. Damien said he'd give me the key when I paid him the twenty bucks I owed him. But every penny I have goes to the save-my-butt-from-Leadpipe fund, so I'm left with no choice but bust the window and climb in.

Damien uses the cabin as a machine shop to fix stuff, mostly boat motors, and as a place to stash contraband. There are drill presses, a lathe, a wizard wand alignment jig, and your basic illegal alchemist's laboratory.

I rifle the cabinets to see what Damien's recently smuggled. Bags of Venusian mind candy. Counterfeit Mercury boots. Bottles of añejo tequila. Jor-Al kryptonite detonators. And a carton of star dust, military weapons grade.

I remember one drunken afternoon when Sgt. Mead taught me how to make a lunge bomb to repel a dragon attack inside the perimeter.

Key words: inside the perimeter.

Mind you, by this time the dragons would've gotten past the spells, the hexes, volleys of magic musket fire, and the dozens of anti-aircraft guns. Using a lunge bomb was the last act of foolhardy heroism before surrender.

The sergeant showed how to attach a can filled with star dust to a long pole—the longer the better—and lunge with the bomb into the open jaws of a dragon.

Crazy rangers. No wonder they stayed drunk. But if the lunge bomb would've worked against a dragon, why not against a water monster?

I arrange the carton of star dust, plus kitchen utensils and empty cans, on a work bench. I screw a bracket to the bottom of an empty coffee can, and in turn slip the bracket over the end of a gondola pole about twenty feet long.

I measure two pounds of star dust into the coffee can. Not enough star dust and I'd only wound the water monster. Too much and I'd blow myself up as well.

I tamp one of the kryptonite detonators into the star dust and cover the end with the plastic lid of the coffee can, which I secure with duct tape. I run the firing wire from the can and tape the wire along the pole. One quick tug arms the detonator. A second tug makes it go boom, hopefully inside the mouth of the water monster.

I become conscious of time. I glance at my wrist, forgetting that I've pawned my watch. The clock on the wall has both hands resting along the bottom of the glass face.

I peer out the window. The tide's come in. The cabin on the next set of pilings rests a couple of feet above the water.

The high tide reminds me that my time is short. My heart catches. Soon, I'll be on the water. Soon, I'll be facing the water monster. Soon, I could die.

I look toward the jetty.

Something huge and pale floats between a derelict trawler and a barge that's foundered on the rocks.

The air is warm but I still get goose bumps.

That something looks like a cross between an orca and a beluga and is the size of two elephants standing tail to trunk. It's the color of a tooth with splotches of gray across its side. The front of the body flattens into what looks like the head of a hammerhead shark.

The water monster.

The goose bumps give way to a chill. I start to shiver.

A layer of clear water sits atop the green murk. The clear water and the sunlight create an illusion that causes me to see the water monster like it's floating in the air. The monster is motionless, except for the dorsal fin waving back and forth, and the chewing of its jaws.

A jetty crab hangs from the water monster's mouth. The crab's shell is the size of a trash can lid. I know the shells are an inch thick and hard as concrete. Yet the water monster munches on the crab and pieces sink and fade into the green murk below.

The hammerhead faces me and sunlight glints off the big shiny eyeballs on each end of the wide, flat head.

The monster keeps chewing, not appearing hungry but as if wanting to keep busy as it waits for me.

How did it know I was going to cross the lagoon?

That chill of fear sinks deep, the warmth of my flesh is gone, and I become ice cold with terror.

I slink from the window and return to the workbench. My fingers tremble as I double-check the lunge bomb. Trembling fingers and high explosives don't go well together so I take a shot, make that two shots, of tequila. The liquor is like a hand on my forehead, warm, soothing, comforting.

Chato buzzes in, a smile with dragonfly wings. "Hey boss, did you see?"

I don't get why he's smiling. "See what?"

"That everything's taken care of." He gestures toward the jetty.

I try to ask but my voice cracks. I start again. "The water monster?"

"What else?" Chato fans his tiny hands. "I got it under control."

I didn't know what "it" was but the last time Chato bragged about an "it," I got into this stupid mess with Leadpipe.

"Yeah, yeah, I get it," I reply. I pick up the lunge bomb and hold it by the long pole. The bomb feels unwieldy, and using it against anything—a dragon, a water monster—is clearly the act of a desperate imbecile.

Chato buzzes over. He asks me what the lunge bomb is and I tell him. He hovers around the can and down the length of the pole. "Crazy idea, boss."

"Did I ask your opinion?"

He shrugs. "Makes you feel better, then keep it. No matter, I got everything under control."

Time to go. My arms and legs are stiff with dread. If everything goes well, I'll be flat broke but alive. If one thing goes wrong, I'll be water monster chow.

I get the lunge bomb and the cigar box with Leadpipe's money. I have to crawl out the window I've broken. I set the cigar box on the deck and lean the lunge bomb upright against the eaves of the cabin roof.

The gondola floats beside the deck, tethered by a bowline looped around one of the pilings.

Chato flies over the gondola. "Hey boss, the boat's pointing to the lagoon. Means the tide's going out. Should make the rowing easier."

"Yeah, yeah, I get it." What concerns me is that with the receding tide, the water's gone completely murky. I can't see more than a few feet into the green haze.

The harbor opens to Enron Lagoon. Pandora Island is a long dark hump on the horizon. Somewhere in all that water, doom waits for me.

Chato sits on a piling. His wings fold behind him. He undoes his shirt to cool off.

"Say boss, you get to the island, it'll be like starting over. No more debts to Leadpipe."

"Yeah, yeah." Starting over. Clean. Until I get in debt again.

I squat along the edge of the deck. I look in the direction of the jetty. The water monster has disappeared.

My nerves tingle as I study the water. I imagine the monster leaping out of the murk and gulping me in one bite. The monster is big enough to smash the cabin off its pilings. If the monster wants me, what is it waiting for?

"Whatcha looking for, boss?"

"Nothing." I don't want Chato to see me get nervous.

I reel in the bowline and examine the gondola. It's shaped like a coffin. I slide the lunge bomb along one of the gunwales and rest the pole gently on the seat. I untie the bowline, hold it in one hand, the cigar box in the other, and hop into the gondola.

The gondola rocks—I get another of the fear shivers—and I crouch low to avoid tipping over. I lower myself into the seat and wedge the cigar box into a space along the gunwale.

In the bow of the boat, there's a box of junk, mostly alchemist supplies: bottles, pieces of alcohol lamps, test tubes, a large bell jar.

I settle into the seat, make sure everything is in place, and grab the oars. I start to row, and the gondola slips from the cabin.

Chato flies to the boat, lands on the stern and sits. He leans against a stanchion and crosses one leg over the other, relaxing like this is some joy ride.

I make long strokes and keep the stern fixed on a point on the jetty. Every few moments I glance over my shoulder toward Pandora Island to make sure I stay on course.

Chato perks up and launches himself into the air. My nerves get sharp.

A white fin rises from the water like a periscope.

My spine seems to melt and I feel my spirit collect around my sphincter. My insides turn to mush and threaten to leak out my butt.

I shake in panic, a blind panic that makes me want to curl on the bottom of the gondola and hide.

The fin approaches. It stands as tall as I am.

I stow the oars. I reach for the lunge bomb. It feels suddenly heavy and clumsy. My mouth goes dry as I think about the foolishness of my plan.

The fin traces a narrow wake around the boat and my breath freezes. The water monster glides so effortlessly through the water that its immense flukes barely disturb the surface.

I rest the lunge bomb across the gunwales.

My nerves jitter. I should've brought the tequila.

Chato buzzes around me, his tiny face pinched in distress. "Whatta doing, boss?"

I don't answer. I just watch the fin.

Chato hovers between me and the water monster. I swat the fairy away. He yells and curses.

I ignore him.

He lands on the stern. "Look, you ain't listening to me. I got a deal worked out with the mere-men. The water monster is not problem if you just..."

"Yeah, yeah, I get it."

Chato beats his wings in fury. "Don't yeah, yeah me, you moron."

I lose it when he says "moron." I swat him, not hard, only enough to knock his minuscule ass against the bow. I'm tired of his second-guessing me.

He lays against the bow plank, looking dizzy and in pain. Well, too bad. I pick the bell jar out of the box of junk and set the jar over him.

I turn my attention back to the water monster. The tide's pushed the gondola past the end of the jetty and I'm floating into the lagoon. I'm close enough to Pandora Island to make out the buildings. Leadpipe O'Brien and his troll gang are probably sitting on a porch watching me through binoculars.

Chato thumps and buzzes against the thick glass of the bell jar. He scowls and hollers about something.

I muscle the lunge bomb hand over hand until I'm holding it by the end of the pole. I wedge the tip of the pole under the seat and tilt the pole up like a mast.

The water monster cruises around me, the dorsal fin knifing through the water, its enormous bulk a white smear in the green murk of the lagoon. On another pass, the water monster arcs its back, and that grotesque hammerhead slices just beneath the surface of the water.

The monster's close, so close I'm scared enough to almost puke.

Chato beats his tiny fists against the bell jar.

The tide pulls me farther into the lagoon. The water monster acts agitated. It swims faster. A wake surges and bubbles behind its powerful flukes. The hammerhead swivels side to side. I wonder why it hasn't attacked yet. Maybe it wants me over the deepest part of the lagoon to share my carcass with baby water monsters.

Carefully, I extend my left arm to hold the pole and lift. The pole rotates and the bottom slides under my right armpit. I swivel the lunge bomb over the right side of the gondola. This way I meet the water monster face-to-face as it circles the boat.

I dip the bomb into the water. The water monster slows and swims around the bow of the gondola. I lever the pole away from me and the bomb scrapes against the flank of the monster.

The force bumps me back and the gondola spins in place. Chato screams and buzzes in the bell jar.

The water monster does a half roll and opens its mouth, a crescent-shape orifice filled with rows of serrated teeth, each as long as my hand.

The sight of those teeth takes my breath and I almost drop the bomb.

The water monster swims away, oblivious that I was about to blow a hole in its side. But I need to put the bomb in its mouth.

I ready the lunge bomb for another try.

Chato screams and knocks his head against the bell jar, but I ignore him.

The water monster makes another pass. The white back breaks the surface, and the hammerhead glides just under the water.

I aim the lunge bomb for the mouth. I tug the firing wire to arm the detonator.

The water monster tilts its head and shows me its jaws. I push the bomb against the mouth. The eye on the closest end of the hammer fixes me, giving an agitated glare as if it didn't understand what I'm doing.

I jab the bomb against the mouth. I have only a few seconds before the water monster swims out of reach.

It opens its mouth, reluctantly as if to humor me, and the bomb snags on those terrible teeth. The pole wrenches out of my hands.

I flail for the pole. My fingers hook the firing wire. I take the last bit of slack from the wire and pull.

The water monster is swimming away when it jerks upward and humps its back. Water geysers upward and splashes me. A loud boom echoes across the lagoon.

The explosion slaps the gondola and about tips me over. I'm tossed backwards and hang on to the gunwale.

Blood stains the water. The water monster floats still, its forward fins drooping, the flukes sagging, the dorsal fin wilting like a melting candle. Slowly, the monster sinks and disappears into the murk.

My fear's gone, and I feel light-headed and giddy.

I look toward the island and put a hand against my brow, shading my eyes. I'm still too far to see anything except for buildings and clumps of trees.

I raise my arms in victory and whoop. "Leadpipe, you fat wart-faced bastard. Did you see this? I hope you bet against me and lost your ass."

I was about to get the oars when I hear: "You idiot. You moron." It's Chato.

The explosion had knocked the bell jar off the bow. I hear Chato but can't see him. His wings beat the water. I rise out of my seat. He's splashing by the hull.

"Hurry, hurry, you moron, before I'm lunch for a carp."

I scoop Chato with an oar. He lies on the paddle, his wings limp, his little chest heaving.

He lifts his head. I expected another string of curses but instead he cries, "Why, why, you fool?"

"What's your problem?" I feel like squishing Chato against the gunwale. "The water monster is dead. I killed it."

Chato tucks himself into a sitting position. He cradles his head in his hands and sobs. "That wasn't the water monster. The mere-men sent it to protect you. As a favor to me."

A surge of water rocks the boat. I turn, bewildered.

The surge pushes the gondola backwards.

A great lump rises from the middle of the lagoon.

My bewilderment turns into shock.

The lump uncurls into something enormous and green and scaly. Tentacles big as telephone poles reach for the sky.

My shock is now naked terror.

Chato stands on the paddle and shouts, "That's the water monster."

Mario Acevedo writes the Felix Gomez vampire-detective series for Eos HarperCollins. Felix routinely battles nymphomaniacs, rogue vampires, alien gangsters, and zombies in his quest for truth, justice, and a better martini. Felix's forthcoming adventures involve werewolves in the wicked city of Charleston, South Carolina. Mario, a past president of RMFW, a nominee for the Colorado Book Award, and RMFW's Writer of the Year for 2009, lives and writes in Five Points, the original ghetto of Denver, Colorado.

The Wind Has Blown the Leaves Away
by William M. Brock

The jacket fit like a glove. Not his style. Rather, if he had a style, this would not be it. The garment was not so much comfortable as comforting, the leather softened by long use and worn to a warm charcoal with brown highlights. He walked between the racks of used clothing to the full-length mirror.

"They get the best stuff from dead people." Larry turned, startled. An old man stood there without a cane or walker—a circus balancing act headed for disaster. His skin, like his brown suit, seemed two sizes too large. Jowls hung like damp rags. With a wheezing laugh, he stepped forward.

Strangled laughter became a genuine coughing fit. "Are you all right?" Larry put his arm around the stick-figure shoulders and helped the old man to a chair. It felt like holding a wounded bird—all bones and heart's flutter. Larry waited beside the chair until the old man could talk normally. "What did you say about dead people?" The jacket began to feel too warm, a little too restricting.

"Living people give away crap they won't wear anymore. And they won't wear a dead relative's clothes. Those end up here, or a place like it." His pale eyes seemed to focus. "Look at the coat you're wearing. That used to be somebody's favorite. It's not just in good shape. It's damn near alive."

The leather had a surface sheen like oil, a butterscotch glow even in the cold fluorescent light. When Larry tried to take off the coat, a loose thread jammed the zipper. As he worked the zipper loose, he glanced at the mirror and saw a stranger's face—unshaven, lined by time and cigarette smoke, eyes as fierce as a desert patriarch's. He turned in time to see an aging hippie type walking away.

A trick of light and motion must have superimposed the man's face on his own. The break with reality disturbed him. "Are you O.K. there, fella? You look like you saw a ghost."

He had forgotten the old man. Sly laughter lurked in the shadows of that voice. Larry felt a little embarrassed, as if caught picking his nose or something equally innocuous and private. The irritation came through in his tone. "Do you have a name, old man?"

"I'm Ladago Culver, Laddie to my friends and enemies. I've been everywhere, done everything, seen it all." He looked down at his hands, age-spotted, trembling. "Hell—now I'm too old to do anything or go anywhere. But I still see plenty."

"Just what is it you think you see?"

"I see a young man in a world of trouble."

"Not me." When Larry shook his head, the coat settled more firmly over his shoulders. "I'm between jobs right now, is all. I'll get by."

Laddie smiled, his mouth wet, toothless. "Is that the good life for you, boy, getting by?" He pinned Larry with that washed-out blue gaze. "Gentle Providence is about to take pity on you, make your life interesting." He gave in once more to that choked laughter, slapping his knee. "And buy the jacket. It'll make a new man of you."

Larry turned back to the mirror. The jacket looked good. He looked taller, stronger, but somehow twisted, deformed.

"I can't wear this. It's … wrong."

"Then you're a lousy judge of right and wrong. Buy the coat, son."

#

"This is a real bargain—red tags are half price today. That'll be $16.18 with tax." The woman at the cash register examined the coat at arms' length. "I hope my grandfather didn't bother you. We let him hang around. The Home is so boring for him during the day." In a stage whisper, she added, "Sometimes he thinks he's a salesman, working here."

"Maybe he is."

On the walk back to his apartment, one sleeve of the coat kept popping out of the bag. After stuffing it back several times, Larry became frustrated and let the sleeve drag on the ground. He felt like Quasimodo stumbling home after the festival, dragging his wonderful hat by one of its bells.

Inside his own door, Larry could relax for the first time that day. A psychologist once called his problem *hyper-vigilance*. The strain of watching everything all the time got to him, especially in the neck and shoulders, and behind his eyes. He took the coat from the bag. On impulse, he checked all the pockets, found nothing but lint, tobacco crumbs, and a hole. He reached through the hole in the pocket with a thumb and forefinger and retrieved two dimes, a penny, and a flat guitar pick from the lining. The pick, sliced from bone or ivory, was yellow with age. On one side was the name *Molly*, written in fine copperplate burned with a hot needle. It felt valuable, lying in his palm—an object of power.

Trying on the jacket again, Larry could not understand his earlier fear. The coat felt great, perfect. He felt perfect, strong, and ready for anything. But he shouldn't be in this room. He should be on the street, checking things out, making things happen. He should drink ouzo and do the goat dance all night long. He caught himself with his hand on the doorknob. This was nuts. He only wanted to eat supper and watch a video.

No one else he knew actually owned a copy of *My Dinner With Andre*. He ate Hormel Chili and peanut butter sandwiches, listening to Wally and Andre solve life's mysteries over potato soup. Tonight, the illusion of company would not work. His mind wandered to the leather jacket, out of sight, but never out of mind.

Enough. Just get rid of it. Holding the bag away from his body, as if it might leak something foul or sticky, he carried it down two flights of stairs to the dumpster. Less jumpy, he felt silly for throwing away money. He fell asleep in the flickering blue television light.

#

And woke in bright sunshine, the pain in his skull a neon ice pick. He couldn't move, or didn't want to move—something might break, might shatter. Where was he? With any luck, a hospital.

He opened his eyes and saw the same familiar room—the television and VCR, the door to the tiny bathroom, the kitchenette in one corner. He wore his most ragged blue jeans. And he wore the leather jacket, the one that should be in the trash.

Taking it off felt like peeling away a layer of skin. He stumbled to the sink and drank three glasses of cold water. Nausea took him to the floor. The headache became bearable. From the smell, whatever happened last night involved a lot of tobacco and whiskey. His feet were black with dirt past the knobs of the ankles—the kind of grime that comes only from walking barefoot through city streets.

He remembered falling asleep on the futon, a vague image—a reflection in muddy water—of his own hand zipping up the jacket. Moving. Running, running, flowing like mercury through the darkness. The dream of that excitement, that thrill, lay beneath pain he felt now.

Reaching for the sink, he felt an odd sensation. Where was his right hand? Another man's hand was attached to his arm. He looked at it with a lotus-eater's detachment. If someone snapped a photograph right now, would it show his face, or another?

The coat yielded a crumpled cigarette pack, and a garish business card:

CRATERS
555-7362 a club 620 Otis
MUSIC
and whatever else we
can get away with

An answering machine picked up on the second ring, the recorded voice a pleasant baritone. "Leo here. Give me one good reason to return your call." Larry broke the connection. What could he say? Hey, Leo. I don't know you, but maybe you saw me in your place? A drunk, barefoot guy in a leather jacket? Last night troubled him like a vivid dream he couldn't remember.

Six-twenty Otis was ten blocks off downtown, twenty minutes by bus and a short walk. What could it hurt to check it out? The thought of bus fare made him think of money. He kept his cash in a video tape box marked *The Treasure of the Sierra Madre*. Apparently sleepwalkers did not need money—not his, anyway. Along with the folded bills, he saw that strange guitar pick. He left it there, afraid to touch it. Before jumping in the shower, he put the coat on the only wooden hanger in his closet. Why bother throwing it away? It would come back, again.

#

The place on Otis had been an auto dealership forty years ago: bricked-in storefront, doors wide enough to admit a '56 DeSoto— early gas station architecture. The doors were solid as a bank vault. Ready to give up, go home, Larry heard faint music down the alleyway.

The alley surprised him. A mural covered the right side of the building. An oriental landscape disappeared into infinity, dotted with gentle people, willow trees, children practicing with wooden swords. It was art, free and on the street, heartbreaking in its beauty. He stared, rapt. A door at the far corner opened with a burst of noise. A woman rushed by, not hurried, just … determined, sure of her destination.

"You should see the other side—it's Hieronymus Bosch with an attitude." A deep scar started below her left eye and cut her smile in half.

Inside the door, the noise reached a killing level. It felt like a giant machine, with rusty sharp-toothed gears grinding away at his brain. A teen-aged girl played keyboards. Close-cropped black hair, face bristling with gray metal piercings, she seemed detached to the point of autism. Larry caught the bass player's attention and mouthed the name "Leo." The musician nodded toward a door across the room, his lips in a slack, buck-toothed smile, eyes floating.

This door was stainless steel, salvaged from a walk-in freezer. Larry entered a bright, clean hallway, mausoleum quiet compared to the practice studio. In the cramped office across the way, a man looked up from punching a calculator. "I think that girl wants to kill her parents with sound. They can't even settle on a name. Last week, Gut Wrench. Today it's Prima Belladonna."

"Gut Wrench is better. Are you Leo? I found this card and—"

"We wondered if you would show up in time. Come on, let's get this mess squared away." Leo stalked off down the hall, a beach ball with pipe cleaner legs and weight lifter arms. Somehow, the man's gruffness did not seem rude or unfriendly. Larry felt compelled to follow.

The hallway looked like an underground service tunnel. He had to duck under water pipes and electrical conduit. "You were expecting me?"

"Hell, yes. Your brother said you're some kind of electronics wizard. That's what I need."

Up three steps, and they were in the middle of a circular room about fifteen feet across. Larry couldn't figure it out. Panels, monitors, and windows of one-way glass lined the curved walls. It looked like the control room for a primitive, derelict flying saucer. Leo hopped over the cables and power cords crisscrossing the floor. Larry followed more deliberately.

Mounted on the wall, next to another door, was a giant blade switch, the kind used to operate the electric chair in old prison movies. Leo had to stand on tiptoe to reach the handle and pull it down. The vast, dark area outside the control room slowly came to life. The ceiling was a cratered moonscape, gray and brown in harsh sunlight and deep shadow. The floor was a shallow bowl, flat black. A planetarium show swirled and rotated across the floor in time to unheard music. A memory struck Larry, stronger than déjà vu, of dancing on the nighttime sky. A long bar curved out of sight against the distant wall. He wondered what kind of people would come to a place like this. People like him, apparently.

Leo spoke up. "You should see it with a thousand people jumping around. The money just flies out of their pockets." He grinned, teeth as white and artificial as his cheap nylon shirt. "The stage is right over our heads. Number three spotlight's been out for a week, and our so-called engineer can't find the problem. Why not see if you can fix it?" He stared at Larry, more challenging than questioning.

To Larry, it felt like a test. He hated tests. There were masking tape labels everywhere, many of them curling or missing. He found a panel labeled "stage lighting." The potentiometer marked "3" was as big as his fist—more at home in a steel mill than a nightclub. It would take a lightning strike to break the damn thing. He followed the cable bundle from the back of the panel, across the floor, behind a cabinet. He saw bits of Teflon insulation, rodent droppings. "Looks like a rat's been chewing on the wires. "

Leo scowled and opened the door. "Morris, get down here. "

"Sure, boss." A young man with a twisted back and aluminum crutches came thumping down the steps from the stage. A white rat with black markings rode on his left shoulder, arrogant as Napoleon on horseback. "What's up?"

"No big deal. But don't let your little friend run loose in here again." He turned to Larry. "Help Morris here splice that cable, then meet me in the rehearsal studio. We need to talk."

Morris pointed to a workbench bolted to one wall. "If you need anything we don't have, go buy it. Just get some cash from Leo."

It took an hour to repair the damage.

Larry found Leo in the practice room, strumming tunelessly on a big twelve string. Without looking up, he said, "Your brother made quite an impression here last night."

The smell of the room made Larry's eyes burn—sweat, smoke, and the earthy, stale odor of something almost dead, or almost alive. He rescued an overturned chair from the floor and sat down. "I meant to tell you before. I don't have a brother."

"Uncle, then? The family resemblance is unmistakable." Larry just gave him a blank look. "Anyhow, he sure as hell knows you. And I've met a thousand poor bastards like him over the years."

"A real derelict, huh?"

"You're kidding, right?" He tossed the guitar and Larry barely caught it in time. "Look at you. Don't even know how to hold that damn thing. Worse than I am. Your benefactor—he called himself Greywolf—sat in that chair last night and played as well as I've heard anyone play. There are two and a half, maybe three people on Earth who could do better. And when I offered him work—good money, too—he turned me down flat. "

"How did he get in here in first place? He doesn't exactly fit the dress code."

"You got that right. People who come here wear rags, but they're outrageously expensive designer rags. We use ethnic Samoans for security." Leo smiled. "Even the graffiti bums give us a wide berth. No one gets past them—except Greywolf. Now don't get me wrong." Leo lowered his voice like a man ashamed of a long-held prejudice. "These Gen Xers are very sweet people. Nothing like the 80s crowd. But after midnight everyone is blitzed. We have to watch close, 'cause anything could set them off. Morris spotted him on one of the monitors. The guy's out on the floor, right under crater Tycho. There is this bubble of stillness around him as everyone stops to look. Call it mime or dance or street theater. It's the damnedest thing I've ever seen. He's like a marionette, a puppet on strings, a tragic figure—crucified, tortured, a concentration camp survivor—like that. But the strings force him into this happy, silly little dance. He ends up tangled up in those imaginary strings, hovering in midair. I saw Nureyev back in '61. *He* couldn't have pulled off that performance. Later, I asked Morris what he saw. He said it was something about a death.

"Whatever the crowd saw, they want more of it. They'll be back again tonight with all their friends; they will be here to see Greywolf do his death dance. And I can't find him. Hell, I don't even know his real name."

To Larry, Leo came off as a compassionate cynic. For all of his talk of money, the man obviously spent little on himself. On the street, he would look like a retired boxer. Doughy shapeless face, long hair, a high forehead—except for the eyes, he could play Ben Franklin. "Maybe I can help you. I think this guy needs me—why me in particular, I don't know."

"Then let's help each other. You get nothing for nothing." Leo stood to leave, as if he had completed some negotiation and only a few details remained to be ironed out. "That abortion of a control room was designed and built by a man named Ian Waterloo, a friend of John Lennon's in the old days. Set up two recording studios for him or some such nonsense. One of the investors insisted we use him." He huffed a little, almost pouting. "I've got investors you don't say no to. Everything worked beautifully for a cross between a snake pit and the set of a horror film. Then he dropped dead, without leaving a single drawing or schematic.

"I need that rat's nest cleaned up before OSHA shuts us down—again. I need a full set of drawings so anyone with half a brain can trace down a problem." He looked off into space, calculating in his head, lips moving to the spin of the numbers. "How about twelve hundred a week for six weeks? After that we'll see, but there's always work to be done. I also own places in St. Louis and Indianapolis."

At the door, he stopped. One more detail had almost escaped him. "Talk to Becky as soon as you can. She wants better lighting for the murals outside."

"Becky? Is that the woman with the scar?" Using an index finger, Larry drew a line from his eye to his chin.

"Hell, we all have scars. Just happens you can see hers."

Larry stood alone in a cluttered room that stank of pain and creation. In one morning, he had walked down a street, turned a corner, opened a door. A new world beckoned. Come. Run away. Join the circus.

He accepted a ride home from Morris, feeling safe in the hand-controlled van. Morris was all right, but his rat was friendlier. Larry froze while climbing the stairs to his apartment. What had happened? He never acted on impulse, never made decisions on gut feeling alone. As a kid, he'd received a bicycle one Christmas, and his first thought was, where's the catch? Today, he took a job, for an outrageous salary, from a peculiar man who collected money and misfits. In the still, bright afternoon, targeted by sunshine, he hurried inside. Drowsing in front of the television, Larry tried to understand where he had lost control of his life.

A knock on the door shocked him out of a daydream. Peeking through the curtains made his heart skip a beat. Her eyes, laughing, stared back from inches away. Becky, the painter from the club. What had Leo said? "Just remember, anything you do could end up in a painting. You'll be walking along, minding your own business, and suddenly see part of your life spread out in front of strangers. Some people find it unsettling."

He meant to explain that friends, acquaintances and strangers were not welcome—to meet him at the club. Instead, she swept right past. "My God! This is worse than my place. Of course, I'm never there except to change clothes." He wanted to throw her out, but she looked strong, stronger than him, anyway. She walked around, red hair a frizzy halo framing her long face, eyes a sponge for detail. "Does Leo know he hired a recluse? Forget it. Leo knows everything."

A little puff of breath from her nose expressed what she thought of Leo's knowledge, or the lack of it. "You're not afraid of heights, are you? Open places? I don't want you to wet your pants if I dangle you off the side of a building or something."

He shook his head. "Nothing like that. A kind of generalized anxiety. It's a lot of work to walk down the street." He looked away, her gaze too steady for comfort. "I have to look for snipers on the roof, assassins in the crowd, open manholes in the pavement, a hundred other things. They are never there, but I have to look anyway." For the first time he really saw her eyes—a color green often found in cats and seldom in people.

This time Becky looked away. "Is that why you don't drink? Relax. I'm not psychic. Just a wild guess. I bet there's nothing in your refrigerator but a jar of mustard."

She read the titles of several video cassettes lying on the coffee table, obviously waiting for a reply. "Sometimes—" He paused. "Sometimes, if I drink too much, I see the things I'm looking for."

"You and a million other people." She laughed, music bubbling from a deep well. "It's just—I can't have you near my paintings if you're some kind of nut. But we all have our quirks, our little ups and downs." She opened a plastic box, revealing the money kept inside.

Too close, too intrusive. He felt real pain, like a fly walking on sunburned skin. "Please leave that alone. It's—"

She reached for the guitar pick, rubbing it between the thumb and forefinger of her left hand. Frowning. "What is this?"

"I found it in a coat I bought at the thrift store. Maybe—"

"Do you mind if I show it to Leo?" He wanted to say, leave it alone, don't touch it—something strange and powerful is happening here. He shrugged his shoulders instead, resigned. She put the object in the watch pocket of her jeans, gave him her crooked smile. "Leo really does know everything, you know."

#

Her van, loaded with compressed air tanks, cans, bottles—all the tools of her work—smelled poisonous, like flammable acid. In answer to his grimace, she said, "I breathe this stuff all day long. Near as I can tell, it's harmless. Mostly acrylic resins and some middlin' powerful solvents. I mix my own colors. The stuff available commercially doesn't hold up outdoors in the city."

"You ever read Lewis Carroll—the Mad Hatter? Hat makers in England went crazy breathing mercury fumes. Think that might happen to you?"

Her eyes flashed bronze with the sunset. "Maybe then I could paint something the critics wouldn't call 'primitive' or 'a throwback to a simpler time.' And those are the ones who like my work."

In the growing twilight, her hair seemed straighter, darker. He hardly noticed the raised scar bisecting her left profile. It seemed part of her, a personal fashion statement.

At the club, she explained the lighting problem. The mural itself astounded him, so he barely heard the lecture. "These ridges—" She used a laser pointer to highlight raised lines that ran through the painting. "Light these at the right color and angle, the whole thing should pop out in three dimensions." He tried to imagine the effect.

The theme of the painting was Sartre's *Hell Is Other People*, but multiplied by ten. At least thirty human figures lusted after things or people they could not have. Up close, they looked like cartoons seen through water. With more distance, they took on a near-photographic reality.

The panel at the bottom left struck him like a hammer blow. A woman in psychiatric restraints, her face a mask of anguish—he could almost hear the white-coated doctor say, "How do we feel today, my dear?"

He looked over at Becky. She went on and on about blue light fanning out over this area, yellow straight down this line. "What are you going to do about the riot?"

She looked at him, alarmed. "Riot?"

"When people trample each other. Running in terror when these things jump off the wall."

She smiled, unabashed. "We'll tear their hearts out." Dimples stood out in sharp relief. The floods overhead cast more shadow than light.

He worked from extension ladders and a window washer's scaffold, mounting small, tightly-focused lights directly to the painting. At three in the morning, groggy from lack of sleep, sick of her shouted instructions and the wino's heckling obscenities, Larry decided to stop for the night. Becky had boundless energy, would never stop short of perfection. She practically danced from one end of the building to the other, eyes reflecting the swirling color of her creation. Joy animated every aspect of her face and body. Larry doubted if he could ever feel so passionate about anything.

Leo came out with three Styrofoam cups of hot chocolate—exactly what they needed. Becky grinned and added an airline-sized bottle of dark rum to hers. Silent, they stood together looking at the mural for a long minute. Leo gave her a fatherly hug. "You know what you've done, here. I've run out of compliments." He looked back at the painting. "Are you sure this ... effect won't show up on television?"

She shook her head. "Takes two eyes to make it work."

"They'll be lined up around the block. And you're about to become very rich. Name your own price for the next one."

"The next one will be better." She was so beautifully alive and breathless, her hair damp with sweat even in the cool night air. Larry felt proud to be a small part of this moment.

Then she handed Leo the guitar pick. "What is it?"

He held it up to the light. "It's a fake."

"A fake what?"

"I mean, even if its real, it's a fake." Leo caught her blank stare, then looked at Larry. Larry shrugged his shoulders. "There were stories, years back, out of Louisiana. Where else? A sixteen-year-old girl with an old woman's eyes and no heartbeat worked magic by writing names on bone, or bits of skin. So even if it's real, it's a fraud. There are no young/old, dead/alive witch-women anywhere, even the delta swampland."

Back in his room, it took Larry an hour to find it, the name *Greywolf* in tiny, perfect letters on the inner right cuff of the jacket.

Before going to sleep, he pinned a note to the collar: NO BOOZE. NO CIGARETTES. AND WEAR SOME GODDAMN SHOES.

#

Larry expected to settle into a routine. Working for Leo, nothing was routine. One "musician" wanted eleven ancient Super-8 projectors to throw noise and flickering light around the stage. Twice, Leo sent him out of town to do work in other nightclubs. Larry finally hired a contractor to redesign the control room. Leo signed the work order without comment.

One morning Larry woke with a copper ring through his eyebrow, the eye still dripping tears from the pain. Another time he woke up with a tiny blue frog tattooed behind his left ear. Other changes were less flamboyant—the apartment within walking distance of the club, never eating alone, no time for movies. There were a lot of people asking for his time. He and Becky became friends, friends too busy to see much of each other.

At twilight, he walked to the club. Becky wanted the lighting on her mural adjusted—again. At times she seemed more like a force of nature than an artist. Rounding a corner, for the first time since that day in the thrift store, he saw the reflection of his dark brother in the storefront glass.

He seemed younger, the lines of his face smoother, hair and beard trimmed, eyes softer, almost tolerant. Larry raised his hand in a tentative wave. Like some sort of magic trick, the refection did the same. They stared at each other in silent understanding. The moment passed, and Larry saw his own image in the water-spotted glass.

Becky was late. He nodded to Ali, and the big man waved him through the door. He looked out over the giant bowl of night. It still disturbed him to come here with the club open and operating. The music plucked at his nerves with icy claws. Each object, every person, seemed sunken in darkness, dappled by starlight, flashed into life by harsh reflections from the moon overhead. They had to drink, had to be high on something.

At the bar, people stood three deep drinking fluorescent blue liquid from plastic bags, expecting free-fall any moment. He saw the girl— small, dark skinned, hair like a sleek helmet, the brightest smile, her eyes… A chip of yellow bone dangled from her left ear, and he thought of the guitar pick. He felt like a shadow among shadows. Her eyes drew him across the dance floor through the maelstrom of flailing bodies and white noise. Most of the dancers wore make-up and clothing that caught the artificial starlight like a silver disease. The music stomped him down, all heartbeat and headache. Choking on the stench of sweat and musk, he reached out for her, drowning.

With a laugh, unheard behind the music, she grabbed his hands and pulled him to her. The faintest suggestion of a scar crossed the left side of her face. The laugh died when she saw the black rose tattooed on his inner wrist, the blue veins tracing out its stem. She placed her own wrist along side of his—the white rose there a mirror image of his own. Together they had the twisted symmetry of an Escher painting done on human flesh. And this girl's eyes were not green, but bits of pale blue a thousand years old.

Her mouth close to his ear, she shouted over the noise and chaos. "Who are you?"

Something in his mind spoke to him. *I am the tree after the wind dies away, the mountain left by the volcano's thunder.* It occurred to him that Greywolf had searched for and found a vacant room, an empty shell to inhabit, until the time came to travel on. He hugged her close, his one heart beating for two, and answered, "That's a choice I have to make."

The voice was his own and not his own.

William M. Brock writes horror and crime noir. His stories have appeared in NFG, Wicked Hollow, Chimera World #1, The Dark Krypt, Nossa Morte, Teddy Bear Cannibal Massacre, *and many other fine Internet magazines, anthologies, and small press publications. He is currently at work on a novel set in the brutal, corrupt shadow world of Mahlon County.*

Lonely Crutch
by Terry Kroenung

Found amongst the effects of Timothy Cratchit, Esq., 1868

Old Marley was dead. Dead as a doornail. That's what Papa told me. Full seven years gone. But he must have meant some other Marley, not the one with his name still inscribed on that awful Mr. Scrooge's warehouse door. That Marley lived... well, in a manner of speaking.

I think I saw him yester night.

My lame leg pained me, so I crawled out of the crowded bed as quiet as I could. Whenever my brothers saw me up, massaging the withered thigh, they always lost their own sleep trying to give me comfort. Glad as I felt for their help, it heartached me when they spent their rest on a lost cause. But we had all been up late, helping Mama to decorate the house, and they snored like locomotives. No doubt they dreamed of another poor but loving Cratchit Christmas in just two days time.

I rubbed the liniment into the dying flesh as if it might do some good. The stinky medicine wasn't half so useful as the firm kneading that worked it into my leg. Papa slaved at the counting house to pay for it, though, so I made a show of applying it. They would all smell it on me, and it made the family feel better about my condition. *Poor things, thinking they know the truth ... thinking there's any real hope.*

If they could feel the weakness spread, feel the mortality creep upward like a preying spider, their hope would have perished. Mine did so long ago. But I kept my knowledge from them, to breathe life onto that remaining spark which they all huddled about, as if it could warm their souls. When I placed my trembling hands together to pray, that is what I asked for. Not more years for me, but more hope for them.

Those thoughts occupied my mind while I tended to that runt of a leg. Since staring at it had never once made it feel better in my ten years on the troubled earth, I looked out the half-frosted window instead. Round and white, like a ripe and moldy cheese, the moon peered back at me … and winked.

The noise of the liniment bottle clattering onto the wooden floor would have startled my brothers awake on any other night. I snatched at my crutch and hobbled away from the upended stool, wedging into the corner of the small room. My tongue dried up like an old raisin and would make no sound, try as it might. Though palsied by terror, I still didn't take my eyes from the window, or from the face that gazed in at it.

For it was a face, of course. Not the moon at all. A countenance as pale as a sad suicide hauled from the Thames, and as transparent as the window of a butcher shop. Hair thin and uncombed, nose long, broad, and flat. Its mouth tight, red, and straight, looking like a wound made by a fiend's blade. No ears visible, due to a white kerchief tied beneath the long jaw and knotted atop the head. Just the sort of cloth that undertakers wind about the faces of the dead to keep their slack mouths from gaping open during the funeral.

At first I thought it a madman, escaped from Bedlam. Or perhaps one of those awful child-snatchers that teacher always warned us of. I feared poor Papa would find my lonely crutch in that corner in the morning, the sole remnant of unlucky Tiny Tim. When that corpse-face pushed its way through the window and into my room, terror wrapped round my thumping heart like a black adder, threatening to squeeze it dead. But as its whole body came into view, my horror gave way to a child's amazement and curiosity.

For the thing did not open the window, nor break it. No, the transparent figure just pushed through the bricks as if stepping through a waterfall.

I wanted to cry out to my brothers to wake and see this wonderful sight. As if anticipating my desire, the apparition put a bony finger to its horrid lips, quelling the wish in an instant. It gave no sign of intending foul play upon my person. In fact, the thing made no move toward me at all, but stood fast to the scrap of carpet next to the bed. *Floated*, rather, for its booted feet did not quite touch the floor. Far from seeming a spirit bent on mayhem, this ghost—for it could naught else—gave the impression that it desired my help, somehow.

Taking the opportunity to survey its whole form, I first made note that it lacked all substance. Looking through it required no effort at all. My visitor might have been made of a bit of fog. Tall and thin, he wore old clothes, from the time of the last King George. A tailed jacket, waistcoat, tight trousers, and tall tasseled boots. His long hair tied back in a pigtail made him look a bit like the Chinamen I sometimes saw below me when bobbing about London on Papa's shoulder. Now I noticed that his spectacles had been pushed up onto his forehead, just as a forgetful accountant might do while hard at work.

No counting-house clerk, though, ever sported the terrible jewelry this one wore. An enormous iron chain, links a hand's-breadth across, wrapped around his middle like some sort of hellish ivy. Held fast to his frame with a padlock that might have restrained an ox, this vine's leaves were heavy cash boxes, giant brass keys, leathern money bags, great wood-bound ledgers ... all the tools of the usurer's trade. My visitor's legs trembled under the strain of so much awful weight.

Putting aside my fear, I asked the ghost, "Is it so heavy?"

His sigh filled the room, like the death rattle of a dying soul. Despite its rumble, my brothers did not stir. "My burden of sin ... could crush mighty Atlas himself." The voice I heard sounded low and dusty, like a desert tomb.

"This is your penance, then?" I whispered, fearful to offend.

"Aye, lad. A lifetime I spent forging these, and for many lifetimes shall I carry them."

I pitied him, no matter my fright, and mourned for all else who might be bound for the same fate.

"You are a spirit, sir?"

The swaddled head nodded. "That I am. The shade of Jacob Marley, neither truly living nor wholly dead. Doomed to walk the earth for an undetermined span, until my lesson be learnt."

With thoughts of the harsh lessons my own schoolmaster gave me by way of his stout stick, I asked, "What lesson is that? And what course of instruction brings you to my bedroom?"

My hair stood up like the needles of a porcupine as the ghost let out such a mournful wail as the miserable damned of Dante might screech. Still my brothers snored, unheeding.

"The soul of every man and woman must journey abroad in life, embracing that of his fellows, adding to their happiness and sharing in their suffering. Those who choose the selfish path must sojourn after their passing, laden down with their wretched sins, witnessing what they did not do." My spirit guest let out a whisper of a smile. "Thus am I arrived, my young Cratchit. The goodness of this house shines out, even amidst London's depravity. Shining souls abide here."

Choosing not to point out how I had dropped a mouse down my sister's shift the day before, I reacted to something he'd said earlier. "Jacob Marley? Would you be the late partner of Mr. Ebenezer Scrooge, he who employs my good father?"

Again the specter sighed, as if reliving a lifetime of regret in an instant. "The same. To my shame, I abetted that wretched man in the smithing of his own dreadful chains." He picked at the padlock on his waist with a long fingernail. "And my own."

"Mr. Scrooge shall follow you in this state, then? When he passes?"

"That he shall. And his burden hung heavier than this many a year ago." Marley closed his cheerless eyes for a moment. "I shudder to think how unbearable it must be now."

I thought of how Scrooge treated Papa and everyone else. "But you cannot mourn his fate, him being such a sour, spiteful man."

"In life I cared naught for the condition of any man's soul, Scrooge's least of all. Heaven knows I paid no heed to my own situation." The phantom shook its head. "But my seven years' journey amongst mankind, as unseen as I had once been unseeing, has been a tonic to me."

Marley sat on the edge of my bed, inches from Peter's blissful sleeping face. My brother took no notice. "I visit him often, you know. Scrooge. He has no more knowledge of my presence than this fine young lad does. I have hoped all this time that Ebenezer would come to purity of his own accord. Alas…"

While he spoke, I retrieved the liniment bottle and resumed treating my leg. It did no more good than it had before, but the habit lay ingrained in me. The spirit eyed my leg, then stared at my face a long while as if he would draw it. After a few moments, he continued.

"Scrooge used to be good, you know," Marley said. "He cared for his fellow man when young. I have spoken to those who knew him then, who are shades now. All are as sad as I at his fall."

Then the spectral remains of Ebenezer Scrooge's business partner told me a long tragic tale of poverty, parental drunkenness, abandonment, loneliness, and loss. Of a friendless boy and an absent father. Of a love gone stale. Of a man who grew so fearful of the world, so afraid of being defeated by it yet again, that he tried to hold it at bay with an acid tongue and a grasping hand. Of a man of so little mirth that he might have welcomed death, save for the dread of what terrors lay in that undiscovered country.

I wiped away a tear for poor Ebenezer Scrooge. A tear, for that miser! I wept for what might have been, and for what a cheerless waste he had become. Looking at Marley's fearsome links, I shuddered to think about what a mighty millstone Scrooge would wear. Might it drag the poor soul straight to perdition, to drown in the lake of tormenting flames?

"Yes," Marley's ghost agreed, as if reading my every thought like a news sheet, "it is too terrible to contemplate, even for him. But what is to be done?"

"Speak to him as you have to me," I suggested with a hiss, rubbing my shrunken limb harder as a spasm of pain tore up it. "Make him see his fate."

"To what end? Scrooge never attended my urgings when I lived. Never once visited me as I lay dying of consumption in that enseamed bed. I coughed my life out quite alone, no reckoning made. And these last seven years, his heart has shrunk to a cinder."

"Other spirits, then. You say you talked with ghosts who knew him. What if many spirits conspired to force the truth upon his mind?"

Marley paused to think, some unfelt otherworld's breeze stirring his wisps of hair. "A possibility. Perchance it would work. We could take him back, to live anew the choices he made." A shadowed pause filled the air with the pangs of a sick-room. "But gaining such cooperation comes at a cost, young Cratchit."

"Cost?" The morbid pain chewed its way into my bowels now.

"To unmake such firm-welded links as Scrooge has made … that requires a sacrifice," the apparition said, seeming to peer into the core of my being. I would have sworn that he tasted my suffering, though I struggled to conceal it. "A pure soul must give of itself."

I caught my breath at that. Despite all that doctors could do, and my family could believe, despite every prayer and every wish, I knew my frail body would give up its own ghost soon. Perhaps in the next year, all that would be left of me would be my lonely crutch in the corner, next to the hearth. That, and an empty place in poor Papa's heart. What would be the great loss in my leaving this vale of tears a wee bit earlier than planned? I, for one, would welcome the relief. As if to accent my choice, a sobbing agony whipped up my spine. This time I could not hide it.

"Such suffering," Marley sighed in a low mournful voice. It sounded like he relived every instant of his last seven years.

"Take me," I blurted, trying to keep from waking my brothers. "My life for Scrooge's redemption."

The phantom's face fell as far as the grave-scarf would allow. "Life … is not enough."

"Not—enough? What else can I give? Spirit, I give it to you, to Scrooge. Accept it. Now." More torture twisted through me. "Please!"

"I wish I could, brave soul. But death cannot buy this gift. It is too easy."

My eyebrows shot up, both from the pain and the astonishment. "Easy? Death is easy?"

"Yes, compared with living…" Marley hesitated. Through him I could see the first rosy hint of dawn through the dirty ice on my windowpane. "…as you are now." I could just hear the whisper he made.

I grasped his meaning at once, despite my tender years. "For Scrooge to redeem himself, I shall not die? May not die?"

The shade nodded, turning a bit to peer out the window.

"For how long?" A spike of fearful woe stabbed my side, not far from my thumping heart.

"As many years as Scrooge has left to him."

Bending almost double, I demanded through clenched teeth, "How many?"

Now Marley's back faced me, his voice no louder than a thought. "Five-and-twenty."

The liniment jar exploded. My agonized hands had clamped down on it with that much force. Both palms suffered cuts. Drops of blood spotted my bare feet. That pain in my side grew worse. Just one thing made it all bearable.

Papa's suffering would diminish.

I hopped about on the cold floor, trying to avoid the broken glass.

Just out of reach lay my crutch, all alone in the corner. If my lonely bargain held, Papa would have to buy a taller one. Perhaps by then Mr. Scrooge would be paying him at his true value. I only knew that I did not dare reveal my secret.

The thought flashed through my pain-addled brain: *Spirit, into your hands I commend … my father.* I thought it quite clever, considering.

At that moment full dawn broke through my frosted window. All my pain vanished like fog in a stiff breeze. So did Marley's ghost. A last phrase touched my ear in that dry voice. "No one may know of our bargain. Adieu. Remember me."

If Scrooge's soul were to be cleansed, it would start at the counting-house. Fewer hours, better salary, more coal in his furnace. A kind word now and then. Perhaps a promotion, a partnership. I saw Mama smiling, my brothers and sisters skipping for joy. Those lines of worry in Papa's face diminished. Presents overflowed at the base of an enormous Christmas tree.

So much love … from a simple bargain. A business arrangement. Interest accrues. Scrooge would approve.

Terry Kroenung has been an infantry officer, teacher on a wagon train, Shakespeare Festival actor, and Chuck E. Cheese. This is his second story involving disturbing doings at Christmas. "Winterlesson," where Santa is shot down by missiles, appeared in Toasted Cheese Literary Journal. *Terry's new fantasy novel,* Brimstone and Lily*, is published by Rare Moon Press.*

Weaving Money
by Liz Hill

With a swish of revolving door, Suzie and I trade the comfort of AC for the shock of steamy city sidewalk.

"Let's make this quick," Suzie says. "Already the sweat's pooling in my bra."

"Quit whining," I say. "At least it's not a maternity bra. A little exercise won't kill you."

Suzie's not happy about it, but we start to walk—well, she walks, I waddle—toward the pedestrian mall a few blocks from our building. Even in stifling heat, it's a relief to be out of the office. Tense, everyone is so tense, trying to feel grateful we still have jobs, trying to stay flexible when we're actually ready to snap like dried twigs. These days our lunch break has less to do with eating and more to do with escape. It's our time to act normal, to pretend nothing has changed.

But even out here the truth is hard to deny. Between the layoffs and the cutbacks, the crowds on the street are sparse. We amble along, window-shopping, laughing at skinny mannequins in unflattering clothes we wouldn't buy even if we had the money. When we pass a toy store, Suzie points out a curly-headed doll in a frilly pink dress.

"Never too soon to buy a baby for your baby," she says.

My feet slow as I pass the doll but I don't dare stop. I'm having a girl, the ultrasound confirmed that. But we still need a hundred necessities: crib, high chair, car seat, clothes, bottles, diapers, the list is endless.

"Sorry, BG," I tell my stomach. "Dolls will have to wait."

"BG?"

"Baby girl."

Suzie rolls her eyes.

"Hey, it may not be original, but it works."

"Have you decided on a real name?"

"We're still debating. Josh has it narrowed down to two, but I'm keeping an open mind." We pass a half-empty sidewalk café. "I have to see her first. To make sure the name fits. Right?"

Suzie looks at me as if I've gone 'round the hormone bend.

"I mean, what if we decide on Hannah and it turns out she's a Kate?"

"She's *your* baby. You get to pick her name."

"You sound like Josh." I tried to explain to him that names have power, that a child's name has to suit her, complement who she really is, deep down. But Josh just laughed and kissed me and told me not to worry so much. That's what Josh always does.

After one more block, the small of my back hurts from walking and I'm dripping with sweat and ready to turn back, but I don't dare complain to Suzie. To catch my breath, I stop in front of a store window overflowing with strange bright things, mostly handmade items. Wood and paper, silk and sticks.

"Third world junk," Suzie says.

"Fair trade," I correct, pointing to the sign above the door. Suzie isn't known for her political correctness.

"Excuse *me*," she says.

The sign promises "unique things from exotic places." There are no exotic trips in my immediate future, and unlike the toy store, I'm pretty sure my wallet is safe here. "Let's just browse," I say. "It looks fun."

"Anything to get out of this heat," she says, following me through the door.

#

The relentless sun keeps watch as the women walk toward their workspace, their sons and daughters tumbling and screeching beside them in the dust. It is early but already the women have nursed babies, tended children, fetched the day's supply of water, and prepared a sparse meal, dividing it as best they could among their families. Now they will turn their attention to the work of weaving money.

Weaving money. This is how it was explained to the tall woman when she first arrived in this place. The women are given plastic and wire, scraps from a factory in the city, to be woven into colorful bracelets and baskets. The suppliers pay the women for their work, then carry these trinkets to Europe and America, where people have a thirst for pretty things and plenty of money to buy them.

Heads bent, fingers flying, the women twist and coax the wire, their fingers raw with the effort. Through the heat of the day they work. Often, to help the time pass more quickly, they sing or tell stories, laughing, pretending nothing has changed.

#

The shop is blessedly cool. The sales clerk glances up.

"Red tags thirty percent off," she says, then resumes text messaging with both thumbs.

Suzie and I wade into a cornucopia of color: pottery and glass, bright scarves and rugs, wall hangings, clothing, beaded jewelry. My hand brushes a blood-red garment, and I lift it to my chest, surprised at its softness, admiring the way it flows. Suzie's brow wrinkles and she shakes her head.

"Not your color," she says.

I return it to the rack. Slits of eyes on a row of wooden masks stare blindly as we pass them on the way to pottery.

"Don't they give you the creeps?" Suzie asks. She picks up a tall cobalt vase, checks the price tag, winces, and carefully sets it down again.

Suzie continues to prowl the store, apparently determined to dislike everything. The hand-hooked rugs are intricate but overpriced, the hand-made jewelry gaudy, the hand-dipped candles crude, the hand-embroidered table runners impractical.

"This is nice." I hold up a placemat woven of rope or straw, striped in graduated shades of gold. "Come feel it."

Suzie holds it between her thumb and forefinger like a tailor appraising cloth. Her nose wrinkles and she moves along toward a wall lined with baskets.

I drop the placemat back into the pile but my palm lingers on its nubbly surface. The colors remind me of my mother's kitchen, how it was my job, every night, to clear the table and wipe my little brother's goop off the placemats. I'd fuss and moan at his mess, the ground-in Spaghetti-o's and blotches of red sauce.

"Be glad that's all you have to worry about," Mom would say. "And that you have the wherewithal to deal with it."

Wherewithal. Where did my mother get a word like that? My nose suddenly flares with the smell of Ivory soap and white vinegar, her secret recipe for fighting stains. They say your nose goes on overdrive when you're pregnant. Maybe they're right. I caress the bulge at my waist, wondering what secrets and pet phrases I will pass along to my girl.

#

The tall woman is very good at weaving. At first, she is proud that the skills she learned from her mother can be exchanged for full bellies and a safe place to lie at night. But she soon understands that her true skills are not needed; there is no time for them here. By day, she works with what she is given, this strange plastic-coated wire. She fashions it quickly into useless pretty things. She keeps pace with the others, though the work is tedious and the hours long. Her hands do their part. But her heart cries out in protest. Every moment she spends on this work seems to threaten something precious, something she cannot bear to lose.

Proper weaving begins before the roots leave the ground. Each stalk is selected with care, with an eye toward its purpose: this basket will carry grain for my children, that one will hold the bread of my brother's family. The carefully chosen stalks must bake for days in the hot sun. And when they are ready, from the first bent stick of a basket's frame, slow, attentive hands weave purpose into every fiber.

But there is no time, here, for such purpose.

"More baskets, more money," the others say. "We must be fast." Fast, fast, they want money fast so they can go to the city and leave this sun-scorched place behind forever.

The tall woman does not want to go to the city. The city has swallowed her brothers and her husband. The city promised piles of money and delivered nothing but loneliness. She runs a hand over the swell of her belly, where the seed of her husband's last goodbye is planted. It is a daughter, she knows this. Last week, when she felt the child's first stirrings, she saw the girl in a dream: small and quick-witted, with her father's laugh and her grandmother's eyes and many, many questions.

One morning, walking for water with the others, the tall woman's sharp eyes seek out what she needs. Two at a time, three, she gathers the stalks. They are nearly weightless, no burden to carry. She lays them to dry in the sun, and she waits, determined.

Her husband's mother scowls at her foolishness. "When we leave this place, what will become of your fine basket?" the old woman spits. "Gone, like everything else."

The tall woman does not listen. It is not that she is without fear. Terrible things happen, as fast as an eye can blink. Beautiful things vanish, but the eye does not forget how beautiful they once were.

#

Something in the shop finally catches Suzie's fancy. "This is pretty," she says, pressing a multi-colored basket toward me. "Feel."

I take it from her and heft its surprising weight in my hand. It's made of wire, of all things. "Heavy," I say, but that's about all I can muster. It's certainly eye-catching but there is something wrong with this basket, something I can't explain.

I set it back on the shelf and another basket catches my eye. Tawny straw, bowl-shaped, this one is deep and coiled so densely it could be watertight. I run my fingers along its smooth round bottom. It feels solid, reliable, yet each strand of reed seems delicate and fragile. How could that be?

Lifting the basket to my nose, I catch the sharp scent of tall summer grass. Maybe my hormones *have* gone insane. How do I know what tall summer grass even smells like? Josh is the country boy, raised in a small town, the grandson of a farmer. The closest I've ever been to a haystack was a drive-by on the interstate.

I sniff the basket again. This time, I can almost smell the dirt it came from.

#

In the evening her fingers ache and she longs for sleep, but the tall woman cannot rest. In the sliver of time before darkness falls, she begins to make a basket for her daughter.

Slowly, with purpose, as her mother taught her, she takes each dried reed and rolls it quickly against her leg to form a strong and perfect coil. As she works, she sings for the girl who swims in her womb, and the song seeps through her skin into the straw and sticks fast, filling every hollow strand with sound.

The work and this song are important. Money will keep them fed. But only this work, this song, will tend the flame of the grandmothers, will keep it burning inside her, inside her daughter. She is building a container of joy, a basket to carry her song.

When at last the beautiful basket is whole, it catches the eye of the man who brings their supplies. "Very pretty," he says, nodding. "Good money." She shakes her head and holds the basket to her chest. "No," she says. "No."

This basket will not go to any trader for any price. This basket is for her daughter.

#

"Are you *sniffing* that basket?" Suzie asks.

"What if I am?"

She comes over to give it a better look; surprisingly, it passes muster. She checks the price tag. "Not exactly a bargain," she says. "But it does seem nicely made. Why don't you get it?"

I peek at the price, exhaling. It's not as bad as I feared. But with less than two months to work before BG is born, we need to save every dime. No matter what I spend, Josh will consider this basket an impulse buy, frivolous, outside our carefully laid plans.

Suzie's twisting the tag around to read the tiny print that lists the country of origin. "Where's that?" she asks.

I shrug. Taking the basket to the cashier, I squint at the world map on the wall behind her. I don't want to admit I have no idea where this place is.

The clerk reaches out for the basket and checks the tag. "Let me show you," she says, smiling as if this kind of thing happened all the time. Her finger taps a small, odd-shaped country. "Right here." On the map it is carnation pink, as if a child has colored it with crayons.

#

Months ago, the tall woman sent word of the baby to her husband, but there was no reply. As the time of the birth approaches, the others reassure her. The men are hard to reach in the city. They are hard at work. She must care for herself and try not to worry.

Though she has borne two sons and knows what to expect, when her time comes, something is different. The pain seems to slice her in two. The women gather to pray, and the elders add their special songs, but still there is only pain and no fine daughter. Even the midwife's practiced hands cannot smooth the way for this girl. And then, just when it seems all the prayers will fly away, taking this child and her mother with them, the news arrives.

The doctor. The doctor!

The swiftest boy is sent but even so, hours pass before the grave-faced man appears. He gives the tall woman medicine for sleep before he cuts the child from her womb.

#

I stare at that small country on the map until it's a pink blur. Then I close my eyes. I can see this basket on my table, piled with fruit, fruit I can almost taste. It's strange how much I want this basket, how much I want this beautiful thing in my home, in *our* home. I check the price tag again.

"This isn't on sale or anything, is it?" I ask.

"No red tag," the clerk says.

No red tag. I start to replace the basket but before I do I lift it to my nose again. It smells like a place I need to be, a place I've never been but have somehow lost.

#

Just as the woman dreamed, it is a daughter, her first loud wail declaring outrage at the world. The doctor clips the cord, stitches the slash and hands the child to the midwife.

The other women pass the infant around, clucking at her beauty, crowing when she sucks greedily. "A strong one," they declare, then bicker over which name will best suit her.

An old woman steps forward and thrusts a basket toward the doctor. "No, no," he says, pushing it back. It is finely woven, solid and lovely, but what will he do with it? He travels from village to village in a small truck. But the woman insists and he knows he cannot refuse. Clutching the basket, he infuses pleasure into his weary voice, promising to use whatever sum it fetches to refresh his meager stock of medicines.

Before leaving, he explains what to watch for. He hopes they understand. Tomorrow, he will not be here to answer their questions.

#

As I slide the basket onto the shelf the baby kicks me. Hard.

"Ooof," I say. "BG's playing soccer in there."

"She's just warming up," Suzie says. "Wait till the game gets underway." She raises her chin toward the shelf. "Not buying the basket?"

I hesitate. I'm not, right? Isn't that what I've decided?

Suzie looks at her watch.

Maybe Josh won't even notice. I can fill the basket with fruit and pretend it was always there.

"Make up your mind, or we'll both be late."

I can brown bag lunch every day, skip my decaf latte, Google grocery coupons, stretch the chicken casserole with rice. But what about the baby? She needs so much, and I want her to have what she needs. I want her to have *wherewithal*. I need to conserve, need to save, need to be sensible.

I take the basket down again and plunk it in front of the sales clerk.

"It's BG's first present," I tell Suzie.

She shakes her head. "I bet she'd rather have the doll."

I'm not so sure of that. I clutch the basket to my chest as we weave our way back to the street, past the masks and the rugs and the beads and the clothes. Before we're even out the door, the clerk is texting again, smiling at her cell phone, paying no mind at all to me or to Suzie or to the small carnation-pink country on the map behind her head.

Liz Hill, a long-time member and former president of RMFW, has had a short story selected for all three RMFW anthologies. She is the co-author of four mysteries for young adults and a non-fiction book, Singing Meditation: Together in Song and Silence *(co-authored with Ruthie Rosauer), due soon from Skinner House Books. Visit www.lizhill.net for more information.*

About Rocky Mountain Fiction Writers

An organization dedicated to the support of writers of novel-length commercial fiction

Rocky Mountain Fiction Writers was founded in 1982 by a small group of novel writers who came together in a quest for support, the latest in market news, education, and access to industry professionals. The needs that brought that original group of writers together have remained constant throughout RMFW's evolution. Today, RMFW has more than 400 members spread across the United States who are focused on mastering the art and craft of novel-length fiction. RMFW has more than 85 published novelists in many genres — romance, mystery, thrillers, fantasy, horror, and science fiction.

RMFW offers four things essential to writers:

First, support for each member, published and unpublished alike. Whether a writer is submitting that first novel for publication or making a best-seller list, members genuinely recognize and applaud the successes of their fellow writers.

Second, education through critique groups, workshops, and the yearly Colorado Gold Writing Contest. Critique groups are the core of RMFW and provide participants an unparalleled opportunity to learn and share with other writers.

Third, access to agents and editors from major publishing houses through the annual Colorado Gold Conference, which is recognized to be one of the best in the country.

Fourth, monthly news and articles through the Rocky Mountain Writer, the official newsletter of RMFW. For more information about Rocky Mountain Fiction Writers and our published authors, visit our website: www.rmfw.org. Hot line phone number is 303-331-2608.

Rocky Mountain Fiction Writers
P.O. Box 545,
Englewood, CO 80151
www.rmfw.org

The Colorado Gold Writers Conference

RMFW hosts a writers' conference each fall, offering authors a chance to get feedback on their works in progress, learn new skills, and meet with some of the publishing industry's top agents and editors. The conference has developed a reputation as one of the best in the country.

Guest speakers include editors from commercial publishing houses, literary agents, well-known authors, and other book industry professionals. Publishing houses that have sent editors to the conference include: Avon, Ballantine, Bantam, Berkley, Crown, Dell, Harlequin, Pocket Books, Silhouette, St. Martin's Press, Tor Books, Walker & Company, and Zebra. Through personal appointments and panels, agents and editors provide writers with excellent opportunities to learn first-hand what publishers are looking for.

In addition to meeting and listening to agents and editors, writers also come to the conference to learn fiction writing techniques and story development craft. Authors share their expertise and experience about all aspects of writing. Past popular panels ranged from homicide detectives explaining how evidence is collected to an herbalist who shared plant lore. Writers in any genre can find workshops that provide information that will benefit their writing careers.

The Colorado Gold Writing Contest

Each year, in conjunction with the Colorado Gold Conference, RMFW sponsors a writing contest for unpublished authors. The contest format prepares authors for submitting their work to agents and publishers, who typically ask to see a "partial." A contest entry consists of the first 20 pages of a novel, exhibiting a writer's style, and an eight-page synopsis, showing how the story is constructed.

Entries are accepted in several genres such as mainstream, mystery, romance, and science fiction (see detailed contest rules). Manuscripts are assessed on the basis of plot, characterization, dialogue, secondary characters, research, etc. The top scoring manuscripts become finalists and are read and ranked by an acquiring editor or agent in that genre. Winners are announced during the Colorado Gold Conference.

The contest is an excellent tool for a writer to get feedback on a work-in-progress. Editors often ask to see a completed manuscript after judging it, and several RMFW members made their first sales as a direct result of becoming a finalist.

Recognition of RMFW Members

The Jasmine Award
Named for long-time member Jasmine Cresswell, this service award was instituted in 1989. RMFW's Executive Committee presents this award to a member who has performed the type of long-term volunteer service and dedication to RMFW epitomized by Jasmine.

RMFW Writer of the Year
Annually, RMFW members vote a published member to be Writer of the Year. Nominees are selected on the basis of the following criteria: participation within RMFW, the quality of an author's writing measured against others within the same genre, and significant professional achievement. To be eligible for the award, an author must have published a novel within the calendar year of the award.

RMFW PEN Award

Awarded at the annual conference to RMFW members who, during the previous year, made the transition from unpublished to published by getting a contract with a commercial publisher.

Published Authors Liaison (PAL)

PAL exists for the purpose of providing networking and promotional opportunities for published authors in RMFW and for promoting RMFW. The feeling among PAL members is that confining membership to authors who have the same needs and concerns strengthens our focus. RMFW members who have published or have a contract to publish novel-length fiction, and did not pay their publisher to publish their book, are automatically members of PAL.

LaVergne, TN USA
20 January 2010
170617LV00004B/45/P